UNMISSING

OTHER TITLES BY MINKA KENT

The Memory Watcher
The Thinnest Air
The Perfect Roommate
The Stillwater Girls
When I Was You
The Watcher Girl

UNMISSING

A THRILLER

MINKA KENT

THOMAS & MERCER

Published by Thomas & Mercer, Seattle

www.apub.com

Amazon, the Amazon logo, and Thomas & Mercer are trademarks of Amazon.com, Inc., or its affiliates.

ISBN-13: 9781542032018
ISBN-10: 1542032016

Cover design by Shasti O'Leary Soudant

Printed in the United States of America

UNMISSING

PROLOGUE

LYDIA

Ten Years Ago

"Don't scream."

It happens in an airtight instant: the hand clamped over my mouth, the warmth of a man's body pressed against my back, the low rasp of a masculine voice against my eardrum.

I writhe and squirm, kicking him in the shins and clawing at his arms, but it only makes him squeeze me tighter, forcing any remaining oxygen from my lungs and rendering me powerless.

"Stop," he says. His breath is hot against my ear as the roaring ocean below muffles his voice.

I contemplate fighting back a second time, freeing myself from these surreal clutches, and making a running leap off the cliff mere yards away. But chances are I'd hit the rocks long before my body reached the turbulent sea. There'd be no surviving a jump like that, and I don't want to die like this—on a tranquil summer day, my new husband waiting for me at home, and my entire life ahead of me.

An hour ago, Luca ran out to gas up the car and grab groceries for dinner, and I left him a note on the kitchen table saying I was going for a hike and would be back soon. I'd have shot him a text, but as per usual, he forgot his phone.

I imagine my husband coming home, placing two paper grocery sacks on the counter, glancing over my note, and waiting . . .

Given that I hike all the time, Luca won't think twice. He will, however, begin to wonder when I'm not back by dusk—but that's hours away.

A lot can happen between now and sundown.

I eye my backpack—one that contains my cell phone and a GPS safety tracker—resting against a nearby tree. So much for being prepared. Twisting again, I thrash and jut my hips against his, but my five-foot-one frame is no match for this man's Herculean strength. My arms are pinned. I don't stand a chance—not without help—and we're miles from any signs of civilization.

Ever since moving to Luca's hometown of Bent Creek, Oregon, a few months ago, I've taken to memorizing these woods from the inside out. Several times a week, I make my way to these trails to be alone with my thoughts; to breathe in the ponderosa pines, earthen air, and ocean brine; and to daydream about the beautiful life we're building.

Luca wants to open a restaurant with an ocean view. I'm applying to nursing school. One of these days we'll start a family—two adorable little Colettos, maybe three. But for now, we're building our dream life one beautiful brick at a time.

If the man behind me thinks I'm going to give that up, he has another thing coming.

"My husband will be looking for me." I force my words through his fingertips, tasting the salt of his sweaty palm. "He knows where I am."

"Shut up." His deep voice tone against my ear sends a chilled spray of goose bumps down my neck. *"Now, I'm going to take my hand off your mouth. You make a sound, you die. Understand?"*

He threatens me with a jerking squeeze.

I nod.

2

I could scream anyway, but this deep into the woods and this close to the ocean, the odds of anyone hearing me are slim, and I'm not about to test this psychopath.

With one arm still gripping my torso against his, he releases his hand from my face and digs into his pocket.

An older woman went missing in these woods not too long ago. It happens from time to time, given that there are hundreds of square miles of wilderness along hundreds of miles of Pacific coastline. Local authorities wasted no time sending a search party, complete with helicopters and dozens of trained volunteers. They ended up finding her three days later, dehydrated, disoriented, and delirious but very much alive. Turns out she'd merely lost her way. These things happen.

I imagine they'll send out a search party for me, too.

If I'm lucky, they'll trace the GPS tracker from my hiker's backpack to this exact location and work their way from there. Regardless, I'll find my way home. I'll do whatever I have to do to survive and make it back to my husband in one piece.

With my heart whooshing in my ears, I steady my breathing and promise myself everything will be okay once I get away from this monster. I know much of these woods like the back of my hand. I could survive days, maybe weeks if I had to. And knowing my husband is waiting for me at home is all the motivation I need to get through whatever it is I'm about to endure.

From the corner of my eye, I spot the man pulling something from his pocket—a white cloth. But before I have time to react, he shoves it over my nose and mouth, his opposite hand gripping the nape of my neck to keep the fabric in place. Fighting back, I hold my breath until it's no longer possible.

Everything goes black.

When I come to, I'm in a one-room cabin with a single blacked-out window, zip-tied to a chair. Alone . . . waiting . . . but for whom and for how much longer is impossible to know.

I yank against my restraints, a vain attempt at freedom.

Thick, hot tears slide down my cheeks, followed by screams trapped behind my duct-taped mouth.

Squinting, I wait for my eyes to adjust before taking in my surroundings. A bed shoved against a wall, no covers. A camper's toilet in the corner. An oversized red Igloo cooler by the door, piled with canned food and a case of water.

Whoever did this intends to keep me alive.

I silence my sobs when the jangle of keys outside the door precedes the slick snap of the dead bolt. A moment later, the door swings on creaky hinges, and the man in the entrance is engulfed by a void of black courtesy of a moonless sky. It has to be nearing midnight by now, which means I've been here nine, maybe ten hours.

Stepping inside with heavy boots, he secures the door behind him, double-checking the locks before resting a lifeless Coleman lamp on the dirty floor. His movements are deliberate, patient. And he hums a haunting tune under his breath.

It's only when he turns back that I'm met with a twisted sneer and a chilling gaze so dark it sucks my soul from my marrow.

I flinch, shrinking into the cold metal chair beneath me.

"Ah, good," he says. *"You're awake."*

CHAPTER ONE

MERRITT

I am—by all accounts—a reasonable woman.

I don't believe in ghosts or the supernatural. I don't subscribe to fortune-tellers, palm readers, or psychic mediums. I don't place stock in afterlife concepts like heaven or hell—which means I certainly don't imagine a person can come back from the grave.

"You must be Merritt." A sunken-eyed, cadaverous figure stands on the other side of my front door. The porch light spills shadows across her gaunt cheeks as a wintry breeze cuts between us.

We've never met, but I've seen enough photos of my husband's first wife to know the face that haunts my occasional nightmares. I'd know those features anywhere—those expressive, heavy-lidded eyes the color of dirt. Her full, perpetually downturned mouth. The ordinary, everywoman features.

I try to respond, but disbelief robs my voice.

I thought she was dead.

We *all* did.

"You don't know me," she says in a voice so docile it disguises her age. Luca's first wife would be around thirty by now, but this woman speaks like a child, subdued and hesitant. As she wrings her hands, her deep gaze widens and pleads, like she expects to be turned away. "My name is Lydia Coletto."

My husband's last name on her lips serves as a jarring reminder of a tragic past Luca and I haven't spoken of since a lifetime ago. I lift a palm to my chest and suck in a February breath that coats my lungs in a paralyzing layer of ice and Oregon petrichor.

The proper half of me considers inviting her in . . . until the flutters of my unborn son in my stomach steal my attention. I place a hand over my eight-month bump, an attempt to comfort us both. Upstairs, our daughter, Elsie, sleeps safe and sound, the projector painting hundreds of tiny stars on her ceiling, accompanied by tinkling lullabies.

Crazy people wander through this town all the time. Drifters mostly. Opportunists. Though it's usually in the warmer summer months when our population nearly triples. There's a homeless camp a few miles down the ocean. Eight miles north is the infamous and controversial Aura Sky Coliving Commune, which tends to draw unconventional types from all over the world.

This isn't Lydia. It can't be.

This is some kind of sick joke.

And this woman, I'm positive, is an opportunistic psychopath.

An impostor.

"I'm so sorry," I say, bracing myself to inject as much courtesy into my tone as possible, deserved or not, "but the woman you're claiming to be died years ago." With a death grip on the doorknob, I force a civil smile. This is clearly an unstable person trying to cash in on a prominent local businessman's personal tragedy. "Please leave now."

She sighs, emitting a foggy breath that temporarily clouds her expression so I can't gauge her reaction. When the condensed air fades into the night sky, her hollowed eyes hold mine with such intention I can't peel my gaze away.

I use the opportunity to take a closer look at her—memorizing everything about this moment should I need to make a police report.

The tattered, paper-thin gray hoodie that hangs off her narrow frame is ruined with stains, and the ripped light-wash jeans drooping from her lower half are at least three inches too short and one size too large. A stained, acid-washed denim backpack sags off one shoulder, and a sock-covered toe pokes out of her left canvas shoe. An assaulting cocktail of unwashed hair and stale cotton invades my nose, sending a wash of nausea through my center.

Behind her, our driveway is dark and the moonlit, seldom-traveled road that stretches beyond our home is vacant. Not a headlight. Not a tire crunching on gravel or bicycle leaning on a kickstand. No friends waiting in the distance behind the needled cover of evergreens. I'm not sure how she got here—or how she plans on leaving.

It's as if she manifested from thin air.

"I'm happy to call you a ride." I steal a glimpse of the oily strands of hair framing her narrow face, realizing they don't stop until well past her waist. She needs a shower. And a meal. Some clean clothes. A haircut. Warmth. Comfort. Professional help. God only knows what else.

Unfortunately, I'm not in a position to be her savior tonight.

"Is he here?" she asks. No name necessary when you're claiming to be someone's dead wife, I suppose.

I don't tell her Luca's out of town this week, which would imply we're home alone. Bent Creek proper is a solid five miles from here, there isn't a neighbor in sight, and the roar of the crashing ocean waves to the rear of the property would drown out the sound of anything nefarious. The nearest security panic button is three rooms from here, and I'm quite certain I left my phone upstairs by the washing machine.

I stiffen my posture—I'm getting ahead of myself. No sense in getting worked up . . . especially when it could hurt the baby.

Clearing my throat, I hold my head high and move the door a few inches closer to the jamb until I can see only half of her. "I'm sorry, but you have to leave or I'll have no choice but to call the police."

The woman peers past me, scanning the twilight surroundings of our foyer, a nonchalant yet intrusive move. I attempt to swallow. If this *is* Lydia, I don't know where she's spent the last ten years or what her life has been like, but I can only imagine the thoughts running through her head as she soaks in the comfortable amenities of the beautiful coastal haven Luca and I have made together.

But I refuse to believe it's her.

It's impossible.

People only come back from the dead in movies and nightmares.

"I need to talk to Luca." The glassiness in her eyes reflects the moon above, and with a quivering lip she adds, "Please. If you had any idea what I've been through . . . how long it took me to get here, to find him . . . I just need to see my husband . . ."

Her voice wisps into nothing, and she swipes at two tears that slide down her haggard cheeks with the back of her hand.

Real tears . . .

She's almost convincing.

This little coastal town attracts all kinds. Old-moneyed. New-moneyed. No-moneyed. Young families. Retirees. Grifters and drifters. Educated professionals and professional-life escapists. We even have a Powerball winner and a handful of B-list celebrities with seldom-used second homes. Bent Creek is a modern-age melting pot, and everyone here has a story.

I'm certain she does, too—but it's not part of ours.

Perhaps she's a failed actor? Maybe she abandoned Hollywood years ago and has been making her way up the coast. Seems like sooner or later those lost souls jump ship and settle around Portland or Seattle. Every once in a while, we catch a few of them here, like fruit flies drawn to a honey jar. And it makes sense—this place is heaven on earth. Relatively affordable, charming, scenic. The perfect place to raise a family. It's the sort of town where locals never leave, vacationers buy property before the end of their first trip, and transients linger longer than most.

"Luca—" she starts to say before I wave my hand to silence her.

"I'm sorry. Goodbye, now." Because there's nothing more to say to this strange woman, I close the door.

A pit forms in the bottom of my stomach, weighing me in place.

I've never closed a door in anyone's face before. Then again, I've never had a reason to.

An unsettled knot remains in my core as I flip the dead bolt, slow and steady. Unmoving, I wait until the sound of her shoes scuffing against my front walk grows fainter, and then I peek out the sidelight window to find pure darkness.

It's almost like she was never there, as if she were a ghost—if a person believed in that sort of thing.

Taking a moment to quell my nerves, I head upstairs to check on Elsie, lingering in her doorway. After I've soothed myself with the sound of her breathing, I triple-check the back door, side entrance, and garage door. Last, I make my rounds through the house, ensuring every one of our twenty-six windows is double-latched and all exterior lights are shining brighter than the sun.

No one's getting in tonight.

Once I make it to my room, I charge my phone and check the security system mainframe. A thirty-second clip of that wisp of a woman ambling up our driveway was recorded at 8:06 PM. I'm not able to determine if she was dropped off . . . or if she walked all this way. Since the camera is motion activated, it didn't capture her until she appeared at the foot of our drive.

I replay the video a half dozen times, fruitlessly zooming in and out, worrying the inside of my lip, attempting in vain to pick up on a detail that wasn't there the first time.

The baby kicks and squirms inside me. Maybe he can sense my unease, or maybe he's reminding me to relax, which has never been my forte—pregnant or not.

With the system armed, I send my husband a good night text. It's three hours later where he is, so I won't disturb him with a phone call, though I'd love nothing more than to hear his soothing voice right now. But I can't bother him with any of this. He's currently in Newark, desperately trying to sell our local restaurant franchise to a national buyer who intends to turn it into a god-awful chain. It isn't ideal, but we've spent the entirety of the last year sinking into the red like quicksand. We don't have a choice. Not selling means we'll lose everything we've worked so hard to achieve. It means layoffs. Bankruptcy. And laughingstock reputations. It means financial uncertainty. And unloading our dream house. It could also incite a change in our relationship dynamics—these things are stressors on a marriage. Put them all together, and it's the perfect recipe for divorce.

Nothing—and I mean nothing—wrecks me more than failure.

Lying in bed, I roll to my side and stuff a pillow between my legs to alleviate the stubborn ache in my hips. Sleep comes at a premium at this stage in my pregnancy, but tonight I'll be chasing it with a fervor.

Unfortunately my mind didn't get the memo, forcing me to replay the entire exchange on a loop in my head. The audacity of that woman to march up to our door at eight o'clock at night. Unannounced. Claiming to be a dead woman. What did she expect? That she'd be welcomed with open arms? That we'd take her word as gold and invite her in for tea?

I sigh and migrate to the cool side of the bed—Luca's side. Once there, I inhale the faint leather-and-vetiver scent of his shampoo that lingers on his pillowcase for a nightly dose of calm. He's my best friend, my person, my *soul mate*. The father of my children. He would do anything for us—literally anything.

And likewise.

There's nothing I wouldn't do to keep them safe—or to keep us together.

Shame on that woman for sticking her nose in someone else's tragedy.

My busy mind fills with a chorus of confrontational words, all the things I wish I would've said to her in that brief, strange encounter we shared. I replay the moment I gently closed the door in her face, and how I was so careful sliding the dead bolt—as though I didn't want to offend her. It's not the level of satisfaction one might seek in this sort of situation, but it'll do.

Restless, I fling the covers off my legs, head for the picture window with the ocean view, and watch the moon rock the waves to sleep. I spend a few minutes steadying my breath . . . four seconds in, four seconds held, and four seconds out—like my therapist taught me years ago, when we were still childless and my anxiety was at a head. But when I'm finished, my heart thuds harder in my chest as my mind is flooded with an alternate concern . . . What if that woman was telling the truth?

What if she's not some deranged charlatan trying to cash in?

What if she *is* Lydia?

From what I know, they had a whirlwind love-at-first-sight relationship that kicked off with a quickie Vegas wedding and ended a few months later with Luca coming home after a grocery run to an empty apartment, no trace of his young bride anywhere. She'd left a note saying she was going out for a hike—something she'd done dozens of times before—only this time she never returned.

A few hours later, Bent Creek police officially declared Lydia a missing person. And as local authorities and volunteers combed nearby ponds, rivers, forests, and beaches, they only managed to locate her hiker's backpack and cell phone—both of which had been tossed over a steep cliff a few miles from the Spearhead trail. Once leads dried up and the tip line stopped ringing, the case went from hot to lukewarm to ice cold in a matter of months. After extensive inquiry by state and federal units, a nationwide search, and a yearlong court hearing, the legal system was satisfied that all investigative avenues had been exhausted and declared her legally dead.

It wasn't easy, but it was the closure Luca needed in order to move on from that strange, cruel tragedy.

Tiptoeing down the hall to my sleeping daughter's room once again, I sweep her into my arms and carry her to our bed. She stirs for a moment, but falls back to sleep the second I lay her on Luca's side and sweep a lock of her baby-fine hair off her forehead.

The earliest years of our marriage were stained with heartbreak, and countless rounds of IVF. When our friends and acquaintances were having baby showers, we were following up with our team of doctors, trying to figure out why the last embryo didn't take. When our friends were posting pictures of wrinkled newborns on social media, we celebrated for them publicly . . . while we privately mourned our losses.

I tried everything—fertility yoga, a strict herbal regimen, wholefood diets, and veganism. I took up running and started seeing a therapist once a week. I downloaded a meditation app. I spent hours poring over infertility forums and obsessing over my cycle.

While those first anniversaries were the hardest, Luca never left my side. He never blamed me for being too stressed or for eating too much sugar. He held my hand through every disappointing ultrasound and every upsetting phone call. And not once did he lose hope or give any indication that he'd experienced enough hardship for one life.

It would've been easy for him to walk away, to find someone who wasn't diving headfirst into her forties and consumed by her maturing biological clock, someone who could give him the family and the happily-ever-after he deserved after everything he'd already been through.

But he stuck by me.

Not that I doubted him for a second.

Luca Coletto is unapologetically loyal, to the core of his soul.

I nuzzle my nose into Elsie's powder-and-lavender-scented neck and listen to her breathe. Cradling the underside of my belly, I make a decision to forget about the crazy woman and to focus on this beautiful life we've crafted out of literal blood, sweat, tears, and an ironclad commitment to one another.

No one—especially not some lunatic wandering off the road—can take it away.

CHAPTER TWO

LYDIA

The handwritten HELP WANTED sign attached to the door of The Blessed Alchemist is sun faded, drooping on one side where the tape has come loose. Either the owner of the shop is picky or no one wants to work here.

Either way, I'm here to save the day.

Hopefully.

The last place I tried turned me away, claiming the position had been filled. Never mind that they left the sign up for weeks. I'm aware that my appearance is off-putting, but all I need is a chance, someone willing to pay me under the table long enough so I can get on my feet until everything comes together.

Adjusting my backpack strap over one shoulder, I step inside. Consumed by an invisible veil of sandalwood, sage, and patchouli, I choke on the thick air, swallowing until the coughing fit subsides. Hollow crystal bells tinkle when the door glides shut. A woven rug beneath my feet says GOOD VIBES ONLY.

"Hello?" I call out when I find the cash register abandoned.

Pan flute music plays from a room in the back. To my left, a wall of vibrant crystals requests my attention. Buckets upon buckets of them. Some raw, some shiny. Each container labeled with feminine handwriting on silver cardstock. *Lapis lazuli. Obsidian. Tiger's eye. Sodalite. Amazonite. Rose quartz. Citrine. Pyrite. Moonstone. Malachite.* There must be a hundred of them.

Moving on, I pass a rack of angel cards with Archangel Barachiel prominently displayed as the "Angel of the Month." *Angel of blessings,* it says.

I could use one or two of those . . .

"Anyone here?" I move closer to the main counter, stopping to examine a display case of evil-eye jewelry before moving to a shelf of various essential oil elixirs, some claiming to ward off negative energy and others promising to elicit true love.

A hollow quartz vessel rests on a stand on the countertop, along with a note that says STRIKE SINGING BOWL FOR SERVICE. I reach for the mallet . . . until a faint voice carries over the music.

A second later, the lace-and-paisley curtains in the back of the shop flutter, and a heavyset woman in a red parka emerges. Her wide stare catches mine, but her thin lips fail to transform into a greeting smile. As she comes closer, I spot streaks of wet mascara beneath her lower lashes.

"Hi, I'm—" I begin to introduce myself and stop when I spot the second woman—this one willowy and lithe, with Alaskan-blue eyes, frizzy white-blonde ringlets, and high cheekbones.

"Can I help you, angel?" she asks with a voice like spun sugar.

My response gets caught.

No one's ever called me "angel" before.

The first lady pushes past me, making a beeline for the door and almost knocking over the angel card rack in the process. I turn and watch her tromp down the sidewalk before ducking inside her gray Mazda hatchback and slamming the door. She flicks the visor down, fixing her smudged makeup before tearing out of her parking spot.

"Is she okay?" I point toward the window.

"Oh, that's just Gloria," the woman says, a hint of a chuckle in her tone. "Comes in once a month for a reading. Apparently she didn't like the one she got today . . . but she'll be fine. Spirit never gives us more than we can handle."

She speaks of "spirit" as casually as a waitress discussing blue plate specials.

I don't let myself react.

I'm not here on some mystical journey, and I'm not here to judge—I'm simply here to get this job so I can find a place to live in Bent Creek and reunite with my husband.

"What brings you in today?" She clasps her hands together and rests them over her heart.

"I noticed the help wanted sign in your window," I say.

Her oceanic eyes glint. "Ah. You're looking for a job?"

I nod. "I'll be honest—I've never worked retail before. But I'm a fast learner. And reliable."

I'd add trustworthy, but in my experience, the only people who verbally label themselves as trustworthy to others are anything but. It's one of those things that needs to be earned, proven, and shown.

"It would only be part-time." She squints, studying me, and whether or not she realizes it, her gaze drops from my head to my toes and back. "Twenty, maybe thirty hours a week? Seasonal, too. Next month things start to pick up, and they don't die down until about September."

"That's fine," I say.

I thought about walking into the temp agency on Landmark Avenue, but given my appearance, I doubted they'd take me seriously. Not to mention, if they were to run my Social Security Number, it'd show up as belonging to a dead woman. While I'm fully prepared to get my life back in the very near future . . . first things first.

Last night I slept in the entryway of the post office on Fifth Street, and as soon as they opened, I bolted for the bathroom, washing my body and hair with handfuls of industrial pink hand soap until I no longer smelled like the outdoors and the musk of unwashed flesh.

This morning I passed a Laundromat, making a last-minute decision to kill some time inside, where it was warm and smelled like fabric softener. It was there I came across a frazzled mother of four who was mumbling under her breath about "assholes who take up dryers." And then I watched in elated shock as she shoved an abandoned load of women's clothing into a plastic basket and placed it on a table designated "lost and found."

Two hours later, she loaded her sticky progeny and clean laundry into the back of her dusty minivan, and I wasted no time rifling through the deserted garb. It was impossibly wrinkled, likely left there for hours, if not all night. Days, maybe. But I managed to snag a complete outfit—and a spare, which I shoved in my backpack along with two mismatched pairs of socks.

I shift on my feet before stepping closer to the Bohemian-esque woman before me.

"I'm Lydia, by the way." I extend my hand. Maybe I should've done that first—introduced myself—but this woman doesn't strike me as formal, so I won't sweat it.

I'm not exactly dressed for an interview in skinny black denim and a baggy leopard-print sweatshirt, but this is better than the ripped jeans and gray hoodie I've been wearing for the past two weeks as I hitchhiked my way up the coast. I only pray she doesn't notice my shoes . . .

"Lovely to meet you, Lydia. You from around here?" She slides her butter-soft hand into mine.

"No, ma'am. From up north originally. Washington State." I opt not to mention that I lived here, albeit briefly, for three blissful months after Luca and I married. It'll only beg more questions that I'm not prepared to answer yet.

"No kidding?" Her thin brows rise. "I just moved here a few years ago myself. Came on a whim after reading some article online and fell in love with the place. How'd you wind up here?"

"Looking to reconnect with an old friend." I press my lips into a tight smile and pray she doesn't ask me to elaborate. "Guess I needed a change of scenery, too."

A business card by the register identifies her as Delphine DuBois, intuitive and owner of The Blessed Alchemist. I've never met someone who claims to be "all knowing" or anything along those lines, but I do believe people exist who are intuitive. And not in any supernatural kind of way. They're simply good at reading people—a trauma response.

"Well if you're coming from up north, I'm not sure the scenery here is all that different from what you're used to," she says with a chuckle.

Fair point.

I pause to collect my thoughts. I need to be careful with what I tell her. If she finds out who I am, it'll be all over town before I get a chance to talk to my husband. I'd hate for him to find out I'm still alive on the five o'clock news.

"I grew up in the eastern part of the state," I say. "We didn't have these pretty ocean views." I keep my answer vague, straddling the truth without giving away too much. I don't want to lie to this woman, but my personal business is my personal business.

Delphine leans over the counter by the register, pushing an ashy incense tray aside and resting her chin on the top of her hand, and sighs. "Nothing quite compares, does it? It's almost paradise here. At least for nine months of the year." She bats a hand. "Anyway, you said you're reconnecting with an old friend?"

"That's the plan." My throat tightens, attempting to choke the words before they come out. "Haven't seen him in a long time. He's not expecting me, so he'll be surprised."

"Nothing like a good old blast from the past," she says with a melancholic half smile. "I'd be lying if I said I didn't fantasize about running into an ex or two every once in a while . . ."

I don't tell her my ex happens to be a married father who has long since moved on.

Not sure our fantasies are remotely congruent.

"Unfinished business." She winks. "I get it. Life is constantly pulling us where we need to go."

"What brought you here?" I redirect the conversation before she asks another question. "Other than the article you read . . ."

"Needed a fresh start." She stands straight, dragging in a long breath that lifts her shoulders as she scans the store. A wistful, closed-mouth smile paints her face. "Born and raised just outside Salt Lake City. Never really fit in. It wasn't until I lost my daughter and my husband in the same year that I decided to start living my truth. We should all get a chance to live before we die, yes?"

"I'm so sorry about your daughter . . . and your husband."

She toys with an opaque green-black stone hanging from her neck.

"Losing my daughter was devastating. Losing my husband?" Her pale brows rise. "Best thing that ever happened to me. He left me for someone else—a married man from our temple, actually. Last I heard, they're shacked up in Costa Rica. Guess they needed to live their truths, too."

All this talk about "truths" sends pinpricks along my arms, but I don't get the sense that it's double-talk or that she's hinting that she knows more about me than I'm letting on. Her eyes are too kind for that, her demeanor too unguarded.

"I'm Delphine, by the way," she says, handing me one of her cards.

I slide it into my back pocket.

"Do you have a phone number?" she asks next.

Lady, I don't even have a bed.

Remaining poised, I shake my head no. "I don't. I'm just getting back on my feet."

Her brows furrow. "Where are you staying?"

I've only been in town a few days. The first night, I slept in a plastic tunnel at the West Grove playground. Night two, I sought shelter in someone's treehouse. Last night was the post office. I've yet to make plans for tonight, but I've had my eye on a plaid sofa someone abandoned in the alley behind the organic grocery mart.

"I don't have a permanent address yet," I say, "if that's what you're asking."

She reads me for an uncomfortable moment before adjusting her posture. "You looking for a place?"

"It's on my list of things to do, yes."

Delphine points to the ceiling. "I rent an apartment above the shop, and I've got a spare bedroom I've been thinking of subletting. It'd be temporary. Just wanted to get a little extra cash under my belt. Been hoping to do some more traveling, but it's hard—running the shop on my own. Plus, I have a cat. If I knew everything would be in capable hands, I'd feel so much better about leaving every once in a while . . ."

Her hands clasp into a prayer position.

"Call me crazy," she says with a sighing smile. And I imagine people do. "But I have a good feeling about you."

"Thank you." I think it's a compliment?

"I think we can make this work." Her mouth twists at one side. "I assume you're available to start immediately?"

I nod. "Ready, willing, and able, ma'am."

She swats an unmanicured hand, all seven of her bracelets jangling. "Please, call me Delphine."

Working her way out from behind the counter, she approaches me with nimble steps, her gauzy dress flowing. And without hesitation, she cups my cheeks in her warm hands and locks her attention on me.

I recoil.

The last person to touch my face wasn't so gentle. In fact, he once squeezed my jaw so hard that a molar came loose. And as my mouth filled with blood, he laughed, but not before forcing me to swallow it all. The metallic taste on my tongue and the gummy hole in my mouth are two sensations I couldn't forget if I tried.

"Oh, angel." She exhales. "You're going to be fine here. Just fine."

My chest tightens, the sensation foreign and heavy. Something brews behind my eyes, but I force it away. I don't allow myself to cry. Personal policy. I learned long ago never to show emotion. It's a sign of weakness. Happy, sad, doesn't matter. Hold your cards close, and no one can use your hand against you.

"You haven't had it easy, have you?" She lets her hands fall from my face.

I release a held breath as she continues to search my face, and then her attention moves to the space around me, as if she's observing something that can't be seen with the naked eye. A chill runs through me, replacing my numbness with temporary tingles.

"You don't have to answer that," she says before I can respond. "There's a heaviness about you. But also a sweetness. You're here on a mission. You're here to do good things. To incite change. I know it. I see it in your eyes."

She's giving me a *reading* . . . I think.

I don't want to offend her, so I give her my full attention, nodding and confirming because I need this job and that room to rent.

Also, she's not wrong . . .

"I appreciate you taking a chance on me," I say, ignoring the fact that this woman is literally hiring me off the street without so much as knowing my last name. To most that would be a red flag, but to someone without options, it's a winning lottery ticket.

I imagine she's lonely, having left her life behind in Utah and migrated out here solo. Back in Greenbrook, Washington, shops like these served as nothing more than junky souvenir stops where vacationers could buy a piece of jewelry or small token to commemorate their mountainside vacation.

"I have some paperwork for you to fill out." She disappears into a back office, emerging a second later with a short stack of forms and a pen with a small geode cluster on the cap.

A cool sweat collects above my brow.

I have my Social Security Number memorized, but I haven't seen my birth certificate since a lifetime ago. And I don't have a license because, as it turns out, kidnapped people have no need for a set of wheels.

"What is it?" She must sense my hesitation.

"I've been off the grid so long . . . it's going to take some time before I can request a copy of my birth certificate. And I don't have a license or a valid ID."

Her mouth bunches at the side. "For tax purposes—and legal ones, too—I really can't pay you under the table."

My stomach drops, heavy and fast, despite being empty.

"But if you can work on getting those things . . ." She speaks slower than before, as if she's weighing risks and benefits. "I'd be happy to take you in. I mean, you're going to need an address, right? Maybe we could swap room and board for some light housekeeping? You could tend to the cat, get groceries, that sort of thing? And in the meantime, I can show you the ropes around the shop so you'll be ready to hit the ground running when you start . . ."

"You'd do that for me?"

"There's a reason our paths crossed today, Lydia." Her tone is convincing, so much so that even *I* believe her sentiment. "You remind me so much of my sweet Amber. I couldn't help her, but maybe I can help you? All I ask is for your complete honesty at all times."

She slicks her hands together, stopping them in a prayer position as she examines me.

"You'd be willing to take a drug test every week, yes?" A motherly tone colors her question as she bats her short lashes. "I have a zero-tolerance policy for the hard stuff."

It makes sense now—my emaciated appearance, my ill-fitting clothes and stringy, unconditioned hair. She must think I'm on the streets because I'm an addict. A lost soul in need of her divine intervention.

I'm a project.

Someone to save.

But I learned long ago that the only person who can save me is . . . me.

I swallow and nod, ignoring the sting of her unintentional insult. "Of course."

"Wonderful."

"I won't let you down," I promise her.

And I mean it. From what I can gather, Delphine DuBois is a saint of a woman with pure intentions and a heart too big for her willowy figure. I have no intentions of causing her an ounce of trouble or being in her way for much longer.

I'm here for one thing and one thing only—to get my life back.

CHAPTER THREE

MERRITT

"How'd it go?" I cradle my phone on my shoulder while lifting Elsie from her high chair, a move that sends a shock of pain down my left shoulder blade. Once again, my body is silently screaming at me to slow down and take it easy.

"Couldn't really get a read on them," Luca says from the other end. "They asked all the right questions, but they weren't overly friendly."

He's wooing not one but three potential buyers for our franchise. If none of them bite this week, things will go from bad to worse the second his feet hit Oregon soil. We'll have to close at least two locations by the end of the month, laying off some of our best, most loyal employees. Not to mention we'll have to dip into our retirement to cover any costs that may come up—as well as living expenses. All this as we prepare to welcome our second babe. These should be happier times.

"Well, that's disappointing." My voice cracks.

"Don't give up on me that easily." The confident chuckle in my husband's voice is planted, but I appreciate his lightheartedness nonetheless. "One down, two to go."

I run a baby wipe across Elsie's face, swiping away the blackberry jam from her morning toast, and then I clean her chubby little fingers one by one. Glancing outside, I spot a couple of moms pushing strollers, gabbing away. As an introvert, making friends—and maintaining those friendships—has always been challenging for me. I kept thinking once I had kids, it would change. I'd find a group of moms to hang out with every week, and I'd finally have my clique.

Only it turns out, mom life is twenty times more isolating than I ever imagined.

At least I have Luca—my best friend, the keeper of my secrets, the knower of my dreams. I'd trade a thousand girlfriends for one of him.

Exhaling, I check the clock above the stove. I've got an appointment with our OB in a half hour, and our part-time nanny should be here any minute. Afterward, I was going to run a few errands—dry cleaner's, post office, baby boutique—before grabbing groceries on the way home. Exhaustion gnaws deep to my marrow today, but staying busy should help keep my mind off that strange woman from last night.

"Change is a part of life," he adds. "This isn't the first mountain we've scaled, won't be our last either."

Three years ago, *Traveler* magazine deemed Bent Creek the "hidden gem of the West Coast," sparking a migration of moneyed Seattleites, San Franciscans, and Portlandians, each one salivating with greed, desperate for unpolluted air, shorter commutes, and heftier bank accounts. The population explosion served us well at first—until we were hit with an influx of shiny, new competing restaurants.

In the blink of a contented eye, our livelihood went from the goose that laid the golden egg to a kamikaze pilot on a mission. From a secret paradise to a brand of pretentiousness I can describe only as sunshine dipped in granola with a side of Patagonia.

"Yeah. I know." I fail to stifle a yawn. My mouth burns from having used Luca's cinnamon toothpaste this morning. I make a note to pick up a tube of mint for myself at the store.

"When was the last time you had a full night's rest?" Luca asks.

I miss my husband, but I must admit the house stays tidier when he's gone. No wayward socks to pick up. No toothpaste to scrub off the sink. No clock to watch while I time dinner with his arrival home in the evenings.

"Hard to get comfortable when you're the size of a house." I'm dying to tell him about the woman because I suspect he'd laugh it off and confirm my suspicions, which would make me feel a million times better—but he needs to be on his A game for these pitches. He needs to focus. And sell. And to do so, he can't be worried about what's happening back home.

"Twenty-four days," he says, referring to our scheduled C-section date. I detect a smile in his voice. "Twenty-four days till we can finally hold him. Think he'll look like you or me?"

He's trying to lift my spirits, and I adore him for that.

"I think he'll surprise us," I say. "It'd be fitting, don't you think?"

After we welcomed Elsie, we were done. My pregnancy with her was difficult and complicated toward the end, leading to an emergency cesarean in which we almost lost her. Fewer things in this life are more traumatic than having a child ripped from your body with blue lips and no heartbeat. Fewer blessings in this world are better than that baby taking her first breath and being laid on you moments after you thought she was gone.

After a handful of tearful conversations, we decided to be grateful for the baby we had, agreeing that we didn't need another one to complete our family.

But this little guy had other plans.

My grandmother once said life is what happens between the curveballs and happy accidents. So far I've found that to be true. But while some may find the uncertainty of life exhilarating, I've always thought it downright terrifying. I've never been a fan of surprises. And my little slice of the world is much more enjoyable when I can control it.

I rub my belly, silently letting him know he's the exception.

The *only* exception.

"What do you think of the name Everett?" Luca asks. An elevator chimes in the background. "After my great-grandfather on my father's side. And it's an *E* name. I know you don't like the whole matching thing, but—"

"I'll add it to the list," I say, opting not to tell him I don't love it. We named our daughter Elsabeth, after my late grandmother. It'd only be fair to honor someone from his side. Hopefully it'll grow on me these next few weeks . . .

From the window above the kitchen sink, I catch the nanny's maroon Kia turning into the drive, though ordinarily I'd hear it from a mile away.

"Annette's here," I say. "I'll text you after my appointment."

I end the call and meet her at the door.

"Good morning, Mrs. C," she says, placing her gas station coffee cup on the marble console, and when she isn't looking, I check to ensure it doesn't etch the stone. "And where's our princess this morning?"

I loathe how she calls my daughter a princess. It insinuates she's spoiled, but I've never said anything because Annette means well and she adores Elsie. That's all that matters. Finding good help in this town, people you can unequivocally trust, is hard, so I choose my battles. Now, if she were plunking my child in front of a television set all day while mindlessly scrolling through her phone, I'd speak up. That's a hill I'd be willing to die on.

A squeal from the kitchen is followed by Elsie's bare feet padding against hardwood. A second later, she charges toward Annette, who scoops her up with open arms. A tight twinge situates in my middle every time I spot the light in my daughter's eyes when she sees her nanny. Sometimes I'm certain it's a hair brighter than the light she gets when she's with me. Then again, it could be my imagination.

It's human nature to assume the worst.

Someone once told me that I'd only be my husband's favorite until we had our first child, and that I'd only be my daughter's favorite until she becomes a teenager and decides she hates everything about me. But I don't think it has to be that way.

I intend to be *everyone's* favorite until my dying breath.

"I'll be back in the early afternoon." I sweep my hair into a high bun, securing it with the elastic on my wrist. I swear it grows an inch a week lately. Coupled with these third-trimester hot flashes, I'm a walking, talking human sauna. "Three o'clock at the absolute latest."

Annette bounces my daughter on her hip. "We'll be here . . . having fun. Right, Princess?"

I restrain a full-body cringe.

"It's supposed to warm up a little today." She speaks to me but looks at my daughter. "Thought we'd play outside a little bit if that's okay?"

Normally I'd agree to that without a hitch—but given last night's events, I'm not sure if that's a good idea.

"Actually, Annette." I clear my throat. "If you wouldn't mind staying indoors today, that'd be great."

She frowns. Confused, disappointed, or both, I'm sure. But it's understandable—this isn't normal for us.

"There have been some solicitors going door-to-door out here," I say. "I don't know if they're from the commune, or if they wandered up the coast and wound up here. Either way, I think we should keep Elsie inside until these people are gone."

Her lips press flat as she digests this. "Why would they come all the way out here?"

Her question is valid—we're miles from town with sparsely placed vacation homes and no actual neighborhoods. True solicitors would have better luck in Bent Creek proper.

"I saw one of them last night." I knead a kink in the small of my back. "Knocked on my door after dark. She was a little rough looking. Kept asking to speak to my husband. It was very unsettling."

Annette shakes her head, validating my concerns. She gets it. "What are they peddling now?" Lines spread across her freckled forehead.

"God only knows." I turn, heading to the kitchen to grab my purse and keys. "All right, I can't be late. Call me if you need anything."

I wait until the two of them are in the family room before double-checking the lock on the front door. And on my way out, I secure the garage entry as well and ensure all our security cameras are online and active enough to pick up the slightest movement. Normally I wouldn't be this vigilant, but after last night, I've no choice but to turn my peaceful oceanside abode into Fort Knox.

I'd rather be safe than sorry.

CHAPTER FOUR

LYDIA

"Home sweet home." Delphine flips the switch by the door of her apartment. A fluorescent light above her kitchen island sparks to life, illuminating a more livable version of her shop.

Same earthy, organic scent.

Same new-age themes.

Less crowded, which is a relief, as I fully anticipated a borderline hoarder situation.

Without question, this place is the Ritz-Carlton compared to the dirt-floor cabin-shack I called "home" for nine years. And it beats sleeping at the post office any day of the week. Anything with running water and an HVAC system is a win at this point.

"It's pretty straightforward." She sweeps a fluffy white cat off the kitchen counter and gently places it on the ground. Without missing a beat, it sashays to me, offers a quiet mew, and stares up with striking yellow eyes. "That's Powder. He was my daughter's cat. Older than dirt now but sweet as can be. You like cats, Lydia?"

I scratch the tip of my itchy nose and pray I'm not allergic. I've never had a cat. Never had a dog either. Not even a guinea pig. I tried to keep a field mouse I found in our walls one time—until it bit my finger when I tried to feed it a moldy Kraft single. I never saw it again after that.

I nod, stooping down to scratch behind Powder's ears. He rubs his head against my hand before weaving between my legs and wrapping his crooked tail around my ankle.

Then he's gone.

"So we've got the kitchen, living room, and dinette here." Delphine makes a sweeping motion as she presents the open floor plan, which includes cabinets painted an unexpected shade of teal and a redbrick fireplace filled with various sizes of white candles. "And down that hallway are two bedrooms and a bathroom. Here, I'll show you where you'll be staying."

I follow her to the far bedroom, a space big enough to hold a twin bed and a chest of drawers. A single window lets in enough light to distract from the low, water-sagged ceiling. The faintest smell of what I can only assume is cat litter lingers in the air. But despite it all, this place is paradise compared to my last accommodation—or any of the ones that came before it. When I was a young girl, home was often a dank basement apartment. A cigarette-scented, roach-infested rental. A storage unit. Most recently, home was a ramshackle cabin. A paint-chipped park bench. The post office . . .

A handmade quilt covers the bed, accented with two fluffed pillows and a mustard-colored afghan throw at the foot. A small lamp with pale-blue fringe gives the room a muted glow, and lacy sheer curtains offer the lone window some dignity.

I'd have loved a place like this when I was younger.

That's all I ever wanted—a mom who could hold a job and a cozy little place of our own. I'd wanted a father, too, but I never wasted too much time wishing for something that was never going to happen. According to my mom, my father didn't know I existed. I was the product of some affair she had with her boss at the Jonesburg Oil and

Lube. And that's what she called me: a product. Wasn't even worthy of a "love child" moniker.

A framed photo by the lamp displays a younger-looking Delphine, her arms wrapped around a gangly teenager with an embarrassed smile.

"That's my Amber." Delphine claps a hand over her heart, head tilted as she studies the photo. "My guardian angel now."

"I can tell she was special." I study the image of Delphine squeezing her daughter tight against her, grinning ear to ear. In the background is a theme park castle—and to the right of the ladies a man has been cut out of the image, leaving nothing but his arm around Amber.

I hope Amber knew how lucky she was to have a parent who actually gave a shit.

Delphine exhales, heading for a closet in the corner. "You know, I kept some of her old clothes. And you are about her size. She was my little twig. Not a lot of meat on her bones. Girl could eat like there was no tomorrow but nothing would stick. I bet you could fit into some of these." She pulls a thin sweater and a pair of narrow, straight-leg jeans from their hangers and holds them up. "I don't know how 'in' these are these days, but you're welcome to wear anything you find in here."

"Thank you." I swallow the lump in my throat that forms in response to the idea of wearing a dead person's clothes. But I'm not in a position to be choosy—only grateful.

"Why don't I finish showing you around?" She places the clothes back on their hangers and shuts the closet, giving the door a good shove with her hips to get it to latch. "This thing likes to get an attitude sometimes." She waves her hand and heads to the hall. "Anyway, here's the bathroom." She reaches inside and flicks on a light. "Just make yourself at home."

Delphine points to a hall closet.

"Vacuum and cleaning supplies are in there," she says. "Towels and extra bedsheets, too."

Delphine strolls back to the kitchen, plucking a handwritten list from beneath a gemstone-turned-magnet on the fridge.

"Think I'll have you make a grocery run today." She hands me the torn sheet of paper. "There's a mart three blocks from here, walking distance. Why don't you get cleaned up and then meet me downstairs? I'll have to get you some cash from the register."

I fold the paper in half. "Sounds like a plan."

Aligning her shoulders with mine, she cups my face between her warm hands, the way she did in her shop earlier. I flinch once more, heart whooshing in my ears. I don't know if I'll ever get used to being touched again.

"I'm so glad you're here," she says, her voice a broken whisper as her eyes well. "Everything's going to work out just fine for you. Know that."

I'm not sure anyone could know something like that.

The future isn't carved in stone—it isn't even written in pencil on the back of a napkin.

But once again, I don't want to offend this gracious woman.

"I'll be downstairs if you need anything," she says on her way out. "Please, angel, make yourself at home."

With that, she's gone.

Eyeing the open bathroom door, I waste little time peeling out of my clothes, grabbing a towel from the linen closet, and filling Delphine's acrylic tub-shower combo with water so hot it turns my fingers pink when I test it—yet another thing I'll never take for granted again.

The Monster used to force me to sponge bathe with ice-cold water—intentionally filling my bucket with ice cubes and laughing as my teeth rattled and my body was consumed with violent shivers.

I was a lab rat to him. An experiment in how much a human could take without breaking. The light in his eyes as he poked and prodded at me reminded me of a teenage boy I once knew a lifetime ago who got in trouble for torturing neighborhood cats. There was a sick curiosity inside him amplified by an inability to feel. People like that do their bidding in the dark, behind closed doors, to living souls incapable of fighting back.

It's why they never get caught.

I locate a jar of lavender and ginseng bath salts beneath the sink and sprinkle in a small handful because I don't think Delphine would mind, as generous as she is. Then I lower myself in, careful inch by careful inch, until sweat beads across my forehead and my body grows used to the intense temperature. I could stay in here for hours. Draining the water every so often and topping it back off. But I won't. I need to grab groceries for Delphine. I need to be a woman of my word because lord knows there aren't enough of us in this world.

Helping myself to a bottle of peppermint shampoo, I wash my hair not once, but twice, relishing the minty tingles that cover my scalp. And then I squeeze a palmful of sandalwood conditioner into my hand and let it sit on my damp mane for five minutes. As my thirsty hair drinks it in, I browse the assortment of body washes in the stainless steel caddy by the tub. I settle on an orange-peel-and-agave option the color of bottled sunshine.

When I'm done, I dry with a thin bath sheet that wraps around my body twice, and I smell like a candy shop. Sickeningly sweet. Headache-inducing. But I'd consider it an overwhelming improvement on the perpetual sweat, earth, and industrial hand soap fragrance I've come to know.

I run one of Delphine's wooden combs through my hair, which is satisfyingly slick and smooth, not a snarl or tangle to be had for the first time in forever. I comb it once more, this time with my eyes shut, enjoying it. Because it's the little things.

Crumpling my dirty clothes in my arms, I carry them to my room, drop them on the bed, and move to the closet to select one of Amber's old outfits. Delphine made a comment about not being sure if these clothes are still "in," but that's the least of my concerns. I wouldn't know what's "in" if it hit me in the face. Before The Monster took me, I never paid attention to trends. And trends aren't exactly a thing when you're living in the wild.

I select a pair of jeans with an expensive-looking label and a name I can't pronounce. Then I layer a threadbare Nirvana T-shirt under a striped Gap sweater and give myself a once-over in the mirror, ensuring my nonexistent pancake breasts are covered. Bras and underwear are definitely on the list, along with shoes and a government ID and all the other items I need to start my life over.

But until then . . .

Heading downstairs to the shop, I find Delphine in the back room, finishing up a reading for some elderly lady clutching a sepia-toned photo of a man in uniform. When they're finished, Delphine collects $100 in cash from the smiling, teary-eyed woman and walks her to the door.

"Here. I'll give this to you." She hands me the cash, which is about half of what I made on my best panhandling day a few months back, before a schizophrenic man with dead, unfocused eyes stole my lucrative spot. "This should cover groceries and any toiletries you need. The grocer is just three blocks north. Oh, and I forgot to put it on the list, but if you could grab a drug-testing kit from the pharmacy section, that'd be great, angel . . ."

She steeples her hands, eyes soft but lips flat.

"Of course." I slide the cash into my back pocket and hit the sidewalk, grateful for the sun overpowering the gray clouds today because I barely need a jacket. And it's a good thing, given the fact that I don't own one.

Ten minutes later, I spot the grocery store parking lot and pick up my pace. But in the midst of crossing the street, I'm nearly taken out by an olive-green BMW SUV that blows through a stop sign and careens into a spot conveniently close to the main doors. A second later, a bun-wearing, lithe woman with a bowling ball for a belly emerges, straightening her square, black sunglasses and securing an oversized tote on her left shoulder.

It takes me only a second to realize it's my husband's current wife.

The BMW chirps as she run-walks toward the building and disappears past the automatic doors.

Delphine might call this divine intervention.

But I call it a lucky break.

Grocery list in hand, I follow.

CHAPTER FIVE

MERRITT

Geriatric pregnancy. Some people get songs stuck in their heads. But today I'm being tormented by a stupid phrase. My regular OB was out, and filling in for her was some ninety-year-old retired physician with giant hearing aids and a white polyester lab coat that had to have been from the seventies. He jammed his cold, gloved fingers inside me, muttered a number I couldn't quite hear, then snapped the gloves off and threw them toward the trash. They fell off the side of the stainless steel bin, but he didn't notice. The nurse took care of them, of course, offering me an apologetic glance as I attempted to sit up from the reclined examination table with zero help.

The doctor seemed fixated on my age, amused almost. As if treating a forty-one-year-old pregnant woman were akin to observing an endangered animal in the wild. I'm sure when he was in the throes of his career, most women were popping out babies a year or two after high school, but times have changed.

Plenty of us wait to have babies until we're older.

And plenty of us wait because we didn't have the choice.

Either way, I'm not the endangered species in this situation—he is.

I grab a shopping cart at the Pine Grove Grocery Co-Op and make a beeline for the produce section. Apparently everyone and their neighbor decided to get groceries at two o'clock on a Wednesday afternoon, because the whole damned town is here.

I wait a patient three minutes for my turn by the onions. And I'm halfway between the bananas and the kiwis, listening to a twentysomething woman in yoga leggings argue with her bearded, man-bunned husband, when I realize I forgot to text Luca after my appointment earlier. Parking my cart, I dig my phone from my tote and fire off a message, letting him know all is well. **Baby's measuring perfectly on schedule. Blood pressure was a little high. They think it's just maternal stress. No protein in urine. Instructed to take it easy. The usual . . .**

The message shows as delivered, but I don't expect a reply. He's likely in a meeting, and I've no doubt he'll get back to me the instant he's free.

I've yet to tell him about the crazy woman last night, opting instead to keep myself busy and distracted. Flitting around town like everything's normal, checking off all my wonderfully ordinary to-do list items is a balm to my frenzied nerves.

And it's working like a charm.

I've thought of that crazy woman only once—and it was a fleeting, passing thought. One that I blinked away with minimal effort.

I fill the cart with our usual produce, adding in a container of dates so I can make Luca's favorite muffins when we welcome him home. I move on to the next items, tossing in a few extras on the way, before ending up in the dairy aisle. I grab a gallon of whole milk for Elsie and head to the next case to grab a quart of the lactose-free variety Luca and I prefer—only that row is unstocked.

Sighing, I scan the other options.

The entire case is sparse.

Obviously someone's not doing their job, which is frustrating because I know this place pays well. They pay so well, in fact, that we've lost a handful of perfectly good employees to them over the years—employees who will laugh with their friends about how they made the right choice as soon as news spreads about our failing restaurants.

My head throbs, and for a fraction of a second, tears brim along the bottom of my eyes.

I'm crying over unstocked *milk*.

And things I can't control.

If Luca were here, he'd tease a smile out of me. He'd remind me how ridiculous this is. And he'd be right. He'd also tell me it's not the end of the world. And once again, he'd be right. I choose a quart of the store-brand version and place it in my cart because it's better than nothing, and then I back my cart out of the corner—only to realize I'm trapped by someone else's cart.

"Excuse me, I—" I begin to say until I'm met with the same dark, sunken gaze from last night.

"Merritt." Her hands wrap so tight on her cart handle that the whites of her knuckles shine through her pale skin. In broad daylight, she's less ghostly than the last time. Her bland brown hair is shinier, combed straight and parted in the middle. And her clothes are clean. Slightly dated, but notably spotless and void of holes or rips. My curious regard falls to her torn shoes—as if I needed more confirmation that she is who I think she is. "Hi."

I consider moving her cart out of the way myself, but my feet are rooted to the floor and my hands, too, grip my cart handle for dear life.

She reaches past, grabbing the closest milk without looking twice at the label because she hasn't taken her eyes off me for a second.

If she were anyone else, I'd offer a polite "hello" and be on my way. But this situation is delicate, and she isn't just anyone else.

She's a deranged psychopath.

"If I didn't know better, I'd think you were following me." I loosen my grip and straighten my shoulders. While she terrifies me, I refuse to give her the satisfaction of knowing that.

"I'm . . . grocery shopping for a friend." Her lips bunch at one side, slow and casual, and she lifts a shoulder to her ear. "Didn't mean to upset you last night."

I arch a brow. "I find that extremely hard to believe . . . having someone show up on your doorstep after dark, claiming to be a dead woman, would be upsetting to anyone. You're lucky you dealt with me and not my husband."

That's not true—Luca is kinder than me on his worst days. But it sounds better. And I want to warn her to stay away, that we're not the kind to mess with.

"I walked to your house," she says. "I didn't realize it was so far from town. Took me longer than I thought. And I didn't want to turn around and walk back because I'd already come all that way . . ."

Part of me wants to ask how she got our address. Luca made sure it was a private listing on the county assessor page, and he had all sales records scrubbed from public real estate listings as well as our name and address removed from search engines. When you're a well-known restaurateur, it's the sort of thing you do to protect yourself and your family.

"You have a lovely home." Her voice is wistful this time. "At least, from what I saw of it. The two of you have really made a nice life together."

I scan our surroundings. For a store as busy as this one, how can the milk aisle be vacant?

Sweat prickles beneath my arms, but I keep my expression frozen and my gaze as icy as the coolers that surround us.

My heart thumps, taut in my chest. "I don't know who you are or where you came from, but—"

"I told you who I am last night," she says with an incredulous squint, and then she rests her elbows on her cart handle, hunching into a comfortable position that insinuates she has no intention of leaving this conversation anytime soon.

"What's your angle? Do you want money? You want to be on the news? Are you obsessed with my husband? What?" I've heard stories of people posting pictures of their beautiful families on social media, gaining followers by the tens of thousands as they let strangers peek into their private life. But that's never been our style. And Luca is nothing if not a private man. He of all people knows there are millions of sickos out there. No need to bait them.

"I want to talk to my husband." Her tone is unsettlingly matter-of-fact. "And I'm not leaving town until that happens, so . . ."

Heat creeps up my neck. My head pounds harder. I imagine my blood pressure is inching into a dangerous zone. This can't be good for me. And especially not for my baby.

This—whatever the hell it is—ends now.

"He's *not* your husband." I reach for her cart, rolling it out of the way, something I should've done the instant we locked eyes.

The sudden movement tips Lydia off-balance, but she catches herself and glances at my items.

"He likes cinnamon toothpaste, not mint. Mint makes him gag. Oh. And there's a pale-pink birth mark on his lower back, left side. Shape of a crescent moon."

My veins crack, ice-cold.

Reaching into *my* shopping cart, she plucks the glass jar of almonds I grabbed by the deli. "And he prefers Marcona—not California. Unsalted. Keeps them in the fridge because he likes them cold."

I try to speak, but nothing comes out.

"He talks in his sleep sometimes," she continues, "but only when he's having a good dream. His favorite childhood memory was when his cousins came from Pennsylvania for a week and they went camping on the beach. When he was eleven, he had an emergency appendectomy." She traces her finger against her torso, drawing an invisible line where Luca's scar would be. "Would you like me to go on?"

She waits, but the words fail to find my lips.

Pushing her cart away she says, "That's what I thought."

By the time I'm able to form a coherent response, she's gone.

CHAPTER SIX

LYDIA

I line up Delphine's groceries on the kitchen counter. Milled cashew butter. Pomegranate seeds. Agave syrup. A block of grass-fed white cheddar from a local dairy. A pound of antibiotic-free deli turkey. Organic gluten-free penne. Ghee. Turmeric. Half a dozen free-range eggs. A quart of oat milk. A new toothbrush for myself as well as a plastic comb, a deodorant stick, and a twenty-pack of elastic hair ties.

Last but not least, a twelve-panel at-home drug test from the pharmacy section.

I peruse her cupboards and fridge, placing things where I think they might go, and I leave the test to sit out by the sink, unopened. A show of good faith. Not that I have anything to hide. I haven't touched a drug in my life. For starters, I could never afford them. And even if I could, I'm pretty sure my mom did enough in her thirty-six years to cover us both for this lifetime.

Collapsing on Delphine's red velvet couch next to her lounging cat, I fantasize about a real fire crackling in her fireplace instead of the vast array of white tapered candles currently on display. Someday I'll have a fireplace. An apartment of my own. Something colorful with warm, soft textures and cozy furniture. Modern plumbing. Heat. Nothing rustic, nothing to remotely remind me of the cabin.

Maybe even a house by the sea . . .

I won't go so far as to say Merritt stole my life, because she had nothing to do with what happened to me, but I can't help but notice the stark contrast between hers and mine.

Who knows how I'd have turned out if it weren't for that fateful afternoon in the woods. Maybe I should be happy for my husband, that he was able to pursue his restaurant dreams without me and plop a pretty little replacement into my spot to boot. But for now, I can't stop focusing on the imbalance of justice. Everything else is background noise.

Powder lifts his head, his yellow eyes homing in on me. And then he hops down and trots to the window, finding a new place in the sun.

A stack of books on the coffee table catches my eye. I'm not sure if they were there earlier. Sitting up, I check them out: a crystal bible, a beginner's chakra guide, and an angel directory.

The authors have various credentials following their names—all doctorates of some kind and then some. Makes them more credible, I imagine. Someone who spends ten years in college couldn't possibly have a marble loose, right?

I chuff.

The power of suggestion is insane, but what's even more insane is that people build entire empires off it. There are millionaires out there who've fattened their bank accounts and secured their futures all because they figured out how to get paid for telling people what they want to hear.

Sighing, I think of Delphine downstairs. Alone. She doesn't strike me as a scammer or an opportunist. Just a woman trying to rebuild her life and put a little good out into the world. My heart aches for the loss of her daughter.

For a woman who puts unquestionable stock in the concept of angels, does she ever wonder where Amber's angels were when her number was called?

Maybe life is easier when you believe in something. I have no doubt my time with The Monster would've been a percentage point or two more tolerable had I clung to the belief that someone was watching over me, planning to rescue me when the moment was right.

But it was only ever me, The Monster, and a million miles of solitude.

No one came.

No one cared.

No one was looking.

He made damned sure I knew that, too—showcasing local newspapers that had stopped running stories about my disappearance, opting to replace that coverage with articles on property tax levies and visits from state senators.

In the blink of an eye, I became old news.

Erased.

Clocking out of my thoughts, I page through the crystal bible, landing on a chapter about carnelians—ugly little red-brown stones said to restore vitality, instill creativity, and intensify motivation. Fitting, seeing as how I came here to get my life back, and I'm going to have to get creative to do so. One could argue my motivation is intense, too.

So that's how this works—confirmation bias. You take a generic word like "luck" or "surprise" or "fortune" or "gratitude," attach it to a stone, and then apply it to whatever scenario matches your current situation.

Easy enough.

I flip to a different section, landing on the page for amazonite—a rock named for women warriors and said to protect the balance between strength and caregiving. If I were a married mother like Merritt, perhaps I'd identify with this one.

I don't blame her for not believing me last night. I didn't intend to show up at her door so late, but I sure as hell wasn't going to turn around and walk five miles to town with nothing to show for my efforts.

Besides, I was hoping my husband would be the one answering the door. He wouldn't have turned me away or denied my existence, that I know for sure.

I wanted him to see me like that—decrepit, homeless, but still very much alive.

In a perfect scenario, the newest Mrs. Coletto would've invited me in and the three of us would've gathered at their kitchen table. Leaving no detail spared, I'd have told them all about my nine years with the man I called The Monster, how I finally escaped, and everything that has led me to this moment.

Reclaiming my life is going to be a backbreaking process, emotionally excruciating at times, but after having been through hell and back, this should be a cakewalk.

I picture Merritt sitting in her state-of-the-art, well-appointed home with her bulbous belly. Her German luxury SUV still warm in the garage from her day about town. The ocean waves crashing outside her windows as the sun lowers in the sky.

I hope she's considering what I said at the grocery store.

I hope she's accepting the fact that I'm back—and that I'm not leaving.

I hope she's contemplating all the ways to make this fair for all involved.

I also pray the next time we run into each other, she'll actually listen to what I have to say—and then she'll bring me to my husband.

Grabbing the stack of Delphine's books, I take them to my new room. I leave the door open because my near-decade in captivity has made me borderline claustrophobic. Tossing the paperbacks on the bed, I head to the window. It's barely fifty degrees out and the thing is drafty as hell, but I crack it a couple of inches anyway to feel some fresh air— yet another thing I'll never take for granted.

I'll likely sleep with it open tonight, too, and under a million covers to stay warm because those are yet another one of life's little comforts

I've gone without for far too long. Even on nights when the wind howled outside the cabin, The Monster would zip himself into a thermal, insulated sleeping bag while I shivered beneath a thin, dirty sheet.

He never liked for me to be too comfortable. He needed to make it clear that the cockroaches in the makeshift kitchenette would be better fed and given more freedom than me.

The Monster said it'd be cruel to give me hope.

I learned early on the difference between cruelty and evil.

I'll take cruelty any day.

I devour the pages of Delphine's crystal bible the way a preteen might devour a book about wizards and dragons. To think that people believe rocks can vibrate and project enough energy to gift their owners with health, wealth, and prosperity is nothing short of fantasy fiction.

The alarm clock on the dresser reads twelve past six when Delphine comes home. Out of respect, I come out of my room and meet her in the kitchen, where she's already preheating her oven. A frozen organic vegetable lasagna rests on the counter.

As newlyweds, Luca and I lived hand to mouth and paycheck to paycheck most weeks, and our fridge was constantly stocked with those ninety-nine-cent individual lasagnas, the kind that smell better than they taste. I grew to love them. Not because they were delicious (they weren't), but because it represented a time in our marriage that we would one day look back upon with nostalgia.

For the first three nights, The Monster didn't feed me. In fact, he'd made it a point to eat in front of me.

It was three months, give or take, before I finally stopped thinking about that lasagna and what it represented.

"Hope you're not starving," she says. "These things are fabulous, but they take a good hour to bake since they're frozen solid. I'd make something else, but it's been a busy day. Didn't have a chance to sit down once. A blessing, though, that's for sure."

I worked in a restaurant waiting tables throughout my late teen years. Mom and I never had much food at home—wherever home was at the time—so I relished the ability to spend eight hours smelling delicious food. It was cheap diner fare. Flash fried and microwaved, mostly. But it was still better than stale cereal or expired condensed soup.

Never did learn to cook.

"I can try to make something," I offer, spacing my words in hopes she picks up on my reluctance.

She waves a hand, bracelets clinking together. "Oh, angel, no. Not tonight. I've already got the oven preheating. I'll take you up on that another time, though."

"I put the groceries away—if there's something you can't find, let me know." I grab an elastic from my wrist and tie my hair back in a long braid that tapers to almost nothing at the bottom. It's well past my hips and in desperate need of a cut. Maybe tomorrow I'll hack it off with a pair of kitchen shears, but today it's the least of my concerns. "I read some of those books you left out. Interesting stuff."

Her mouth stretches wide, and her eyes twinkle. "Isn't it?"

"That's moldavite, right?" I point to her necklace, the jagged green rock dangling from a tiny silver pendant. If I'm not mistaken, it's a piece of meteorite said to be fifteen million years old—not a true crystal, but people tend to treat it just the same. That "bible" said it's one of the most powerful change-inciting rocks a person can own and advised that it wasn't a "beginner" stone.

"You *are* a quick learner, aren't you?" She twists the pendant between her thumb and forefinger, flashing a sheepish grin. "I shouldn't be wearing it as much as I have been lately. I know better."

I wink. "Secret's safe with me."

"Guess I've been in a rut." She exhales, staring over my shoulder with a blankness in her eyes. "Asked the universe for a change, to point me in a new direction. And then four days later, you walked in. Four is my sacred number." She shrugs like she's sharing a verified fact. "Do you ever find yourself seeing repeating numbers?"

"Never." For almost ten years, I didn't see a clock, a book page, a deck of playing cards, or a car license plate. I dreamed of them, though—for a glimpse of something ordinary, something outside those four brown walls.

Her rosy lips press flat. "Pay attention and you will. Signs are all around us, all the time. But you have to be looking, or you won't see them."

The oven beeps, and she wastes no time sliding the block of frozen lasagna across the middle rack.

"Oh, angel, would you mind taking care of this quick?" Delphine takes the drug test off the counter. She places it in my hands, cupping hers over mine and letting them linger for a tender moment, a silent apology perhaps.

Whatever makes her feel safe around me . . .

"I'll be right back." I disappear into the bathroom and come out with a clean sample two minutes later.

With gloved hands and the dip sticks spread across the counter over paper towels, she processes the test with the confidence of someone who's done it a hundred times before. I watch, chewing the inside of my lip despite having nothing to be worried about.

A few minutes later, Delphine hums a pleased note. "Perfect. Absolutely perfect. I'm so proud of you."

My lips part as I almost tell her I've never done drugs in my life, but I abort that mission because the point is moot.

Delphine collects the supplies into a small trash bag and cleans the counter before snapping off her latex gloves and tossing everything into the kitchen wastebasket.

"I was thinking." Her back is to me. "Maybe tomorrow we could get you a cell phone? Maybe one of those prepaid ones since you don't have ID? You definitely need something, though, angel. I'll need a way of reaching you when I'm not at the shop. Plus, it's just not safe in this day and age to go without a phone."

I had a phone the day I was taken . . . in my backpack . . . tragically out of reach. Despite having that "lifeline," I'm still standing here with her. Still rail thin. Still sporting more scars on my body than I can count. Still missing a molar. Still some wandering homeless woman gazing into the warm, glowing windows of my husband's manse.

"I talked to my friend this afternoon," Delphine continues. "She works at the vital records office at the courthouse. Said it could take a few weeks for your birth certificate to come in. Could take even longer to get your Social Security Card—but you'll need your birth certificate to get that. It's a whole process. But once you have both, you'll be able to get an ID. Maybe even a driver's license, if that's something you're interested in?"

It's been a decade since I sat behind the wheel of a car.

I wonder if I'd have to learn all over again, or if it'd be like riding a bicycle.

"I know it seems like a lot of steps, but we'll take it one day at a time, one *thing* at a time," Delphine says. "It's all we can do, really. Just know you're not alone."

I lean against the counter, watching Delphine flit about the kitchen, talking nonstop. She fills the cat food. Waters five plants by the kitchen sink and two by the living room window.

Plants are simple, requiring only water and sunlight and a little bit of air.

These plants live a better life than I ever did.

I wonder how it would work—getting a copy of a birth certificate or any government ID for that matter—after a person's been legally dead for years.

I haven't tried—in fact, I didn't know I was "dead" until shortly after I escaped last year. I'd been aimlessly wandering around some hole-in-the-wall township up the coast when it started pouring. Heading into a library for shelter, I came across someone's abandoned library card next to a bay of computers. Scanning the badge, I signed on under a stranger's account and proceeded to google myself with quivering fingers.

The timer on the computer was set for sixty minutes. A nearby sign stated users had to request additional time from the checkout desk—obviously not an option for me given the fact that the woman on the forgotten card was easily three times my age.

But for sixty minutes, I hoovered article after article about that fateful night, the days that passed, then the months, and finally, the years. Beyond the article announcing I'd been officially declared dead after a suspicious disappearance and dried-up leads, there was nothing.

It all stopped.

I was a local sensation—and then I was a dead woman.

"Are you anxious, angel?" Delphine asks. "You keep cracking your knuckles."

I hadn't realized.

The Monster used to hate when I'd crack them, so I'd hold off in his presence, counting down the minutes until he would leave so I could release the pressure. It was the closest thing I ever had to physical pleasure.

I can't do any of this until I talk to Luca. If Delphine's friend at the vital records office catches wind of my return, it could get back to him before I have a chance to see him first.

"Do you like tea?" Delphine plucks two mugs off a rack before I answer, and then she fills a black-and-white checkered kettle with ionized bottled water. "Have a seat at the table, we can have a little chat while we wait for dinner to finish."

I hesitate, though she doesn't notice.

Being told what to do—specifically when I can sit, when I can stand, and when I can eat—takes me back to my time with The Monster. But I remind myself Delphine is not a monster . . . not even close.

My throat is tight and my shoulders are tense, but I gather a deep breath and take a seat while she prepares our tea.

"Oolong or herbal blend?" she asks. "I have a lovely berry and hibiscus you might like?"

Choice. The Monster never gave me a choice. Yet another way Delphine is nothing like him.

"Berry and hibiscus sounds perfect." I wait for my tea.

Tonight I'll have to think of ways to stall the birth certificate. In the meantime, I'll steer the conversation and keep her talking about herself. Most people love to talk about themselves. The Monster did. It was his favorite topic. He'd wax on for hours about how intelligent he was, how he was the only person in his family line worth a damn. How he was going to "be someone" someday.

I learned early on that if I kept him talking about himself, he'd forget to make my life a living hell. Or it'd delay it until later, when he was too tired to be brutal, too preoccupied with his delusions of grandeur to stay hard long enough to finish.

"So you grew up in Utah?" I ask when she places a jade-green cup in front of me. I turn the handle to find the image of a woman in some kind of meditative pose on the other side. Eyes closed. Smiling. Blissfully unaware. Reminds me of Merritt in her seaside abode. I bet she meditates.

"Cottonwood Heights." She takes the chair across from me, which creaks as she settles in. "Ever heard of it?"

"Sounds familiar," I lie. We never traveled when I was a kid, so I never bothered taking an interest in maps outside of school.

"Pretty town." Delphine takes a careful sip. "Mountains everywhere you look. Not far from the city if you wanted some good shopping or restaurants. Great place to raise a family if that's your priority. Wonderful schools. Plenty to do."

I studied Amber's picture earlier, the one in the frame in my room. She seemed like the sort of person who skirted the edge of normal. Not quite pretty enough to run around with the cheerleaders and jocks, too scrawny and awkward looking to hang out with the cool kids. Overplucked, mismatched brows. An abundance of dark eye makeup. Hair colored an unnatural shade of box-dye blonde. In a single photograph, I could tell she was dying to be anyone but herself.

Maybe in another life, we could've been friends.

For the hour that follows, Delphine tells me everything I could ever need to know about her hometown—and then some. And when we finish our dinner, I excuse myself to my room with a "headache." I hate to lie, but I need to be alone with my thoughts, and I can take only so much Cottonwood Heights.

Cracking the window a few more inches, I gather a lungful of the crisp air before climbing under a pile of covers. And while Delphine tinkers around in the kitchen, I think only of my husband.

Eyes closed, a hundred reunion scenarios fill my mind, playing like movies on my lids.

The life I was always meant to live is finally within reach.

And it's going to be glorious.

CHAPTER SEVEN

I place a sleeping Elsie in her bed and find myself in the kitchen, staring at the jar of almonds on my counter. I'd grabbed them for myself on a whim, in passing. But I remember now, those early years of our marriage when Luca would eat cold, unsalted Marcona almonds like there was no tomorrow—and then one day he just . . . stopped. No explanation.

Only someone from his past could've known something so nuanced and mundane.

I place the almonds in the pantry before pulling up the internet browser on my phone and googling *Lydia Coletto*.

I get 243,000 results.

Burying my face in my hands, I collect myself enough to brew a cup of chamomile and get settled on the family room sofa. Confined in the dark, throw blanket over my legs and my tea cooling on a coaster beside me, I nosedive down a rabbit hole I never thought I'd visit again in my lifetime.

The first several pages are fruitless, nonsensical, or irrelevant.

Narrowing my search to *Lydia Coletto missing woman* chops the results into a more manageable list, but it still takes me a solid half hour to find an archived article from a now-defunct website and a decade-old write-up from a local news station.

I don't waste precious time reading the articles—I already know what happened, and I know it directly from the horse's mouth. What I'm interested in are the photos. A small gallery of images fills the page halfway through the article. All of them are lower quality, clearly taken on a cheap cell phone from that era, many of them taken at the seaside diner where she and Luca first met.

Lydia grinning in a green waitressing dress with a brown apron . . .

Lydia dipping a crinkle-cut french fry into a chocolate malt . . .

Lydia cheesing to the camera in her colleague's chef hat . . .

Add ten years and subtract twenty pounds maybe, but her features match the woman from today. I can't convince myself otherwise, even if I wanted to.

Everything about Lydia—then and now—is average and unremarkable. Tragically forgettable. And that's what everyone did.

Her search was a local sensation for a hot minute . . . and then people moved on.

They *always* do.

Luca moved on, too.

He couldn't have lived in the shadow of his past the rest of his life. That wouldn't have been fair to him. He did his due diligence as a spouse. He searched for her in accordance with Oregon's evidence-of-death statute, placing notices in national papers and collecting as much evidence (circumstantial, concrete, or otherwise) as he could to prove she was never coming back. It wasn't until the court system declared her dead years after her disappearance that he felt he could so much as think about marrying someone else. To top it off, their entire relationship was a blink-and-you'll-miss-it situation. They were young and impulsive. A quickie wedding in Vegas, and they were off to the races.

Luca hadn't known her but a handful of months before she vanished.

The entire thing was a nightmare for him—all the man wanted was to grieve quietly and move on, to no longer live in the shadow of what might have been.

It's possible there were things he didn't know about her past, things he couldn't possibly have gleaned in such a short amount of time.

I study Lydia's face a few minutes more, darken my phone, and slump back into the pitch-black stillness of this room.

My attention is possessed by a picture window I've walked by a hundred times, one that presents a view that takes my breath away no matter the time or day or season of the year. It's the reason we bought this house. That and the privacy. Over the course of a year, what started out as a midnineties nightmare with hunter-green and burgundy wallpaper and a forest's worth of oak trim transformed into a serene daydream of a home. Bathed in natural light, with creamy walls and chic furnishings, I couldn't have wished for a more perfect place to grow old with Luca.

The beautiful vision past the window fades away. I no longer see the moonlight painting crashing waves or the thick trees that protect and enshrine our property to the north and south. I don't eye my daughter's playset—the one Luca designed from scratch and had custom built. Nor do I notice our beloved miniature greenhouse or the swing bench we've rocked on while reading book after book to Elsie.

All that remains is a deep, dark, endless void of night sky.

I married Luca knowing I was his second wife, well aware of what happened before we built our life together. But nothing could have prepared me for this. And not knowing what happens next for us, for our family . . . is unnerving.

Terrifying in its own way.

There isn't a precedent for this sort of thing. For now we're stuck in this murky gray area between doing the right thing and preserving what remains of the life we've built.

Breaking out of my trance, I wake my phone and pull up the local news. Not a single headline mentions that a formerly missing woman has been found. Lydia—wherever she's been—must have come here first. A move that suggests she wanted to see Luca before anyone else . . .

I toss my blanket aside and winch myself up from the sofa. I carry my untouched tea to the kitchen and dump the cooled liquid down the sink. Wasted, unappreciated, gone forever.

I worry my life will hold the same fate once Luca learns his first wife has come back for him. It's only a matter of time before he learns this, and while I should be the one to tell him, every time I try to form the words, they get stuck.

Once I'm settled into bed, I text my husband a quick good night and my nightly reminder that I love him, lest he forget. It's a word that wasn't often spoken in my household. In fact, I distinctly recall mustering up the courage to say it to my father at my mother's funeral. I didn't think he heard me the first time, so I cleared my throat and said it again. Louder. His response? *Yes, Merritt. I heard you.*

My phone vibrates from the nightstand as a call from Luca lights my screen.

"You're up late," I answer.

He exhales into the receiver. "Can't sleep."

An icy blast cracks through my veins and my exhaustion fades, replaced with a quick jolt of adrenaline. What if he knows? What if she found his number and called him? What if he's hiding from me the very same thing I'm hiding from him?

I sit up and position a pillow behind my back before resting against the headboard. "Need to talk about it?"

"Just wanted to hear your voice." His hotel room TV drones in the background, hardly enough to distract from the underlying dissonance in his tone.

I want to know what's really on his mind.

I also *don't* want to know.

"That's all?" I manage a teasing chuckle, trying to keep this light.

"That and I'm just thinking about tomorrow's presentation." A yawn paints his voice. He could fall asleep if he'd let himself, I'm sure. "Going over the last one in my head. Trying to figure out what I could do differently this time."

Rolling to my side, I fixate on the five-by-seven family photo on my nightstand. I chose every outfit in that shoot, from the kelly-green tie hanging from Luca's neck to the antique diamond dahlia pendant dangling from mine. It had to be perfect—and it was.

It's dark in here, but I make out the outlines of our exuberant faces. Even if I couldn't, I have the image memorized by heart. It's one of my favorites—taken the week after we found out we were going to be a family of four and a month before our accountant informed us things were worse than we initially were told.

"I'm glad you called." I slide the frame off the table and tuck it under my pillow. For now, I'll soak up these last moments of pretending like everything's normal and nothing's wrong.

Lydia's return is going to change things. Though for better or worse, it's impossible to know yet.

Only one thing is certain—the second my husband gets home, our lives are never going to be the same.

CHAPTER EIGHT

LYDIA

"Good morning, angel. Sleep well?" I find Delphine doing yoga in the living room shortly after eight o'clock the next morning.

The overpowering aroma of freshly brewing coffee mingles with the cocktail of new-age scents already permeating the air, and my stomach furls.

"Hope I didn't wake you. Tried to keep my music low . . ." She dials down the volume on her Bluetooth speaker before stretching her arms behind her back. "Oh, and I'm so sorry. I was thinking we could hit up the vital records office today, but I just checked my website, and someone booked two back-to-back sessions for this afternoon."

She offers a sympathetic pout, studying my face.

"It's fine," I assure her, swatting a hand and swallowing the relief that bubbles up from my center. I didn't know we were moving full speed ahead on the government ID thing. I'm not sure what I'd have said had she sprung that trip on me.

One thing at a time.

Placing a cupped palm over her heart, she exhales. "Thank you so much for understanding. Are you a coffee drinker, angel? Help yourself. I made a little extra because I wasn't sure."

Minka Kent

I never drank coffee until I became homeless and realized I could seek refuge in a warm diner for an hour or two for a mere buck and some change. A little extra for a tip. It was bitter at first. Hard on my seldom-used, sensitized stomach. But eventually I grew to associate it with comfort. I'd go so far as to say I learned to like it, deeming it an affordable luxury.

The mind is a powerful thing.

"There's some almond milk creamer in the fridge if you don't take it black." She contorts her body into a new position, threading one arm beneath the other as she bends at the waist. "So I was thinking . . . I'll probably have you do some laundry for me today." A whistled exhalation passes through her lips as she moves to the next pose. "You know, I always used to hate doing laundry when I had a family. It was just this never-ending chore. I'd do three loads, and four more would pop up. Like Whac-A-Mole but with dirty clothes. Anyway . . . now that I'm only doing it for one, it's kind of depressing."

Delphine just might be one of the loneliest souls I've ever met. Not that I've met a lot of lonely souls. But hers practically oozes from her porcelain pores. It colors every word that comes from her mouth. It makes sense why she latched on to me the way she did, so trusting and desperate at the same time.

She rises, folding her hands into a prayer position. Closing her eyes, she mutters something under her breath, so faint I can't make it out from this side of the apartment. And then she disappears into her bedroom. A second later, she emerges with two overstuffed canvas drawstring bags and a roll of quarters.

"Our facility's in the basement." She places everything on the kitchen table. "But the washer's out of order. Landlord keeps saying he's going to fix it, but you know how that goes." She rolls her eyes. "Anyway, there's a Laundromat about five blocks west of here. Bright-blue roof. Right on the corner. You can't miss it. Hope that's not too far for you to walk?"

The bags look heavy, and I'm used to traveling light, but five blocks is nothing compared to the hundreds of miles I've logged these past six months.

"Not at all," I say.

"Wonderful, angel. When you get back, come find me in the shop, and I'll find you something else to do."

I wait until she leaves before getting cleaned up and heading out. While I know exactly which Laundromat she's referring to, I take a longer route, soaking in the sunshine and fresh air and keeping my eyes peeled for a familiar face or two . . . because I certainly won't run into my husband—or his wife—staying cooped up in that apartment all day.

CHAPTER NINE

MERRITT

I'm going mad. Not angry-mad, but crazy. The clock on the dash blinks to 12:01 PM, informing me I've been driving around town aimlessly for three hours now. I've scanned every sidewalk, peered into every shop front. I've crept past every public park and slowed down by every bus bench. I even called the homeless shelter in the next town over—no one knew of a woman fitting Lydia's description.

I have half a mind to head to the Aura Sky commune, but I've heard they don't appreciate unexpected visitors.

I need to find this woman before Luca gets home. I need to get to her first, find out what exactly she wants. Understand her expectations. Try to get ahead of the storm. I hate to assume the worst, but every time I close my eyes, I picture a media frenzy. Photographers outside our door. Journalists begging for an interview. My child screaming out of fear. Restaurant employees being harassed for insider information. Perhaps it's an overreaction, but there are so many ways in which this could go. This isn't the sort of thing that happens around here. Around anywhere, really. Most dead people stay . . . dead. Curiosity from the general public would only be natural—but I'm not about to allow my family to become the center of some entertaining *Dateline* special.

We're nothing if not private people.

Annette's with Elsie for two more hours. I called her in on her off day on short notice, fibbing about some unexpected doctor's appointment when I sensed hesitation in her tone. Thursdays are normally reserved for her grandkids, and I feel awful about taking her away from them, but desperate times and all . . .

Lightheaded, I pull into a parking spot outside The Coastal Commissary. I head in for a decaf latte and a turkey avocado wrap. My blood sugar is bottoming out. I haven't eaten since this morning, and even then I couldn't swallow more than two bites of blueberry oatmeal before my stomach threatened to expel it into the kitchen sink.

I consume my lunch in the car in record time, picking stray bits of lettuce off my undulating belly and tossing them out the window for the birds. And when I'm done, I continue on my mission, keeping a close eye on the time.

Thirty minutes into the next leg of my journey, my gas light comes on. Flicking my turn signal, I hook a sharp right and pull into a corner Chevron to top off my tank. It's only when I'm leaving that I notice a stick-thin woman hauling two bags on her back. Her hair billows in the wind with each step, long and stringy and down to her hips. I lift my foot off the brake and head her way.

As soon as I get closer, I slow down to get a better look.

It's *her*.

I pull into a parking spot a half a block up, roll down my passenger window, and wait for her to get closer.

"Lydia," I call out when she's within shouting distance. "Lydia, hi."

I catch her stare in the side mirror, and she makes her way to my car, dropping her bags with two heavy clunks on the sidewalk.

I lean over the console. "I'm so glad I saw you . . . Wanted to tell you I'm so sorry about the other day. I was wondering if you had some time to talk?"

I nibble my thumbnail—an old, anxious habit. One I broke Luca of many moons ago, a hypocritical yet necessary move.

"I won't take up too much of your—" I begin to say when she opens my rear passenger door and shoves her bags in the back.

Without a word, she climbs in beside me.

I hold my breath, half expecting her to smell unkempt like she did the first night, only I'm met with a peculiar combination of peppermint and oranges. A hint of patchouli, too.

Leaving the car in park, I rap my fingers on the steering wheel and take a deep breath.

"I'm sorry I didn't believe you," I say. Though the tiniest sliver of me still doesn't—maybe because I don't want to. "I was just wondering if you could tell me what happened?" She's quiet, her attention heavy and sinking into me like invisible teeth. "I don't understand. We—Luca—thought you were . . . deceased."

I muster the courage to make eye contact with her and end up distracted for a moment, hypnotized by the abyss of her dark gaze.

Folding her skeletal hands in her lap, she focuses over the dash, at the back of the parked Camry in front of us.

My whole life, I've never trusted quiet people; something about their busy brains and all the things they *aren't* saying makes me nervous.

"It's a long story," she finally says.

"Begin anywhere you'd like." It's a strange thing to say to someone in her situation, but then again, this entire situation is strange. "Or I can begin, if you prefer? I can tell you what I know?"

"No offense, but this isn't about you." Her words bite, but she has a point.

"I just didn't know if it would make it easier for you to talk to me." I keep my pitch delicate. I don't know if she feels threatened by me, by my position in Luca's life, but I want her to know I'm here to listen. Plus it's imperative we start this out on an amicable front, or things could get ugly, fast.

"Do I look like a person who has trouble talking to people?" Her words are matter-of-fact and her tone is neutral. But her eyes are so vacant that her gaze sends a chill through my backside despite the heated seats beneath me.

The answer is yes. Nothing about her screams friendly people-person. But I keep that to myself.

"I'm sorry. I didn't mean to offend you." She looks like a lot of things, all at the same time. Unstable. Broken. Capable. Determined.

"It's okay. It's not like you're slamming a door in my face again."

I can't tell if she's joking . . . I don't think she is?

"I apologize for that, too," I say. "It was dark when you showed up. And you were claiming to be a dead woman. I'll be completely honest, it terrified me."

Lydia smirks. "That doesn't seem like it'd be all that hard to do. You seem . . . uptight. Not what I expected for Luca."

I pick at a hangnail for a fraction of a second. I'm in desperate need of a manicure, but who has time for self-care when my entire world is upending?

"We're quite the opposites, aren't we?" I ask.

"You and Luca? Or you and me?"

"Both . . . I guess." I cringe on the inside, praying I don't offend her. I know what people see when they look at me, and I've always divided them into two groups: those who aspire to be like me and those who find themselves triggered, as if everything *I* have somehow prevents them from having everything *they* want.

"To say the least." Lydia scans the shiny buttons and knobs of my dash and console before settling her attention on the polished screen with its showstopping radio and navigation display.

This vehicle is over the top, embarrassingly so. No one needs a Swarovski crystal gear shifter, heated and cooled cup holders, hand-gesture functions, a sky lounge of twinkling lights, or massaging seats, but Luca picked it out for me for my fortieth. He put a lot of time and effort into choosing it. Plus, he knows how much I loathe spending hours upon hours haggling at car dealerships. It was a thoughtful gift all around.

"You're older than him," she says. It's not a question.

"By a handful of years, yes." And by "handful," I mean five. But it's not something I tend to advertise because people do the math and insert uncomfortable scenarios such as envisioning myself at fifteen and Luca at ten. They ignore the fact that we met when we were both adults. "Why?"

"Just an observation."

Lydia herself was not yet twenty-one when she disappeared, which means she's thirty. I have a sister about her age—Adair. While we have nothing in common besides eye color and we live on opposite coasts, I've no doubt that if I went missing, she'd make a million waves until I was found, and she'd be calling in every three-letter agency in the country plus Scotland Yard.

That was one of the more tragic things I remember about Lydia's disappearance—she had no family. She was an only child. Her father wasn't in the picture, and her mom passed away from sepsis when Lydia was eighteen—likely a result of using contaminated street needles. Luca, local authorities, and some random Facebook group of Nebraskan true crime junkies were the only ones who looked for her.

"I think we're getting off track here," I say, dialing down the heat because my car has morphed into a sauna. "Why don't you just start from the beginning? And tell me everything that happened?"

"Shouldn't Luca hear it first?"

I hesitate. "Yes. He should."

"So let's go to him."

I bite my lip. I hate to tell anyone I'm alone, but there's no getting out of this now.

"He's not available," I say.

She frowns. "Where is he?"

"Working."

"Then let's go to him. Surely he can spare a few minutes for his wives, don't you think?"

The flippant ease at which the word "wives" slips off her tongue sends a sickening trill down my spine, but I don't react in case it's what she wants.

Lydia lifts a brow as she awaits my response. Two nights ago she was so fragile, delicate as vintage china. Today there's a quiet air of confidence about her.

Is it an act?

With palpitations in my ears, I clear my throat and straighten my shoulders. "He's actually out of town."

Lydia points to my phone in the cup holder. "Then call him."

He has another pitch tomorrow—the third and final. Now is not the time.

"This is the sort of news he should find out in person . . . Why don't you come by on Saturday? Is eight o'clock too late? I'd like to have my daughter in bed first, so we can give you our full attention." I place a slight emphasis on *we* and *our*, letting her know that we're a united front.

I don't know if she intends to drive a wedge between us, but while her situation is gravely unfortunate, a handful of months together and a quickie marriage to Luca aren't going to trump the years we've spent building our life together.

"I'll be there." With that, she climbs out of my car and grabs her things from the back.

I collect myself as she walks off, bags slung over her frail frame, and then I drive home—trembling the entire way.

CHAPTER TEN

LYDIA

"I take it this is the friend you were wanting to reconnect with?" It's pouring when Delphine pulls into my husband's extralong, extrawide driveway and parks in front of the fourth stall. Her wipers swish and screech across the windshield as Neil Diamond croons an uplifting tune from her tinny speakers—a nod to simpler times.

"It is." I prop the hood on the leather jacket I found in Amber's collection and tuck my hair back so it doesn't get wet.

Earlier Delphine gave me a kitchen cut per my request, chopping my hair into a blunt style that stops just below my shoulders. It's a flattering length, making my fine strands appear bouncier than before—not that I give a shit about that kind of stuff. This isn't a beauty contest, and if it were, Merritt would beat me by a landslide with her glossy, highlighted ash-brown locks, her blinding-white, straight teeth, those full lips and dimpled chin, and her crystal-clear blue eyes unfairly accented with a fringe of dark lashes.

She may be older than him, but she's poised and sophisticated. Quietly elegant, like someone who grew up on the East Coast attending boarding schools and becoming proficient in dressage and Latin. The kind of woman who turns heads and accepts free drinks from smitten men who want nothing more than a moment of her attention.

How Luca went from me to Merritt is a mystery I intend to solve—if only for the sheer curiosity of it.

"You have your phone, right?" Delphine points to my jacket pocket, referring to the prepaid wireless flip phone she gifted me two days ago.

"I do. Thanks for the reminder." I pull it out to show her. I don't yet have the number memorized, but Delphine said it had three sevens in it, which meant it was lucky. "Not used to carrying one of these."

She places her hand over mine. "Text me when you want me to pick you up, okay? I programmed my number in there so you'd have it."

The motherly tone in her voice almost shatters my heart for a myriad of reasons, but I force the sensation away. This isn't the time or the place to get emotional.

"Good luck, angel." Delphine squints at the exterior of my husband's well-lit look-at-me abode, and her lips tuck down at the corners.

I almost question whether she's getting bad vibes, until I realize how ridiculous that sounds. I've been spending way too much time in Woo-Woo World.

Making a mad dash for the front door, I skip over puddles in my holey shoes and seek cover under their front stoop. Clearing the tightness from my throat, I press the doorbell and then rest my ice-block hands in my pockets.

The moment of truth awaits.

My fingertips quiver, and my knees weaken.

Memories of the last time I saw my husband flood my mind.

I'm not the same person I was when he knew me.

We're strangers now.

I tug my hood down and fix my hair. I want to look decent, but not too decent. I don't want to underplay all the terrible things I've gone through. I don't want to seem too well adjusted—because I'm anything but. I deserve all the sympathy and compassion my husband has to offer, and I won't feel a sliver of guilt.

He's the reason I survived.

And the only reason I'm standing here.

The door swings open, and warm air floods the stoop, enveloping me like an invisible hug.

"Lydia, hi. Come on in." It's only Merritt.

My heart lurches from unmet anticipation. If it could come out of my body, it'd have landed in a wet plop at my feet.

She steps out of the way, her floral silk kimono billowing with each graceful sway of her pregnant hips. Jet-black leggings cover her long legs and a tight, white maternity tank top conceals her protruding bump. Her shampoo-commercial mane has been curled, and when she smiles, I spot a hint of lipstick on her mouth. A nude pink. Brushing past me, she leaves a faint trail of department store perfume.

I envision her standing in her fancy bathroom, fussing with her hair and slicking on a tasteful coat or two of lipstick—but it doesn't seem logical. This isn't the kind of thing a person dresses up for. Then again, she strikes me as the nervous type. Maybe this is her way of getting a handle on some aspect of the situation?

She can't control what's about to happen to her life, but at least she can look pretty . . .

Or maybe she wants to assert her place in the hierarchy.

The beautiful one.

The refined one.

The one who bears the literal fruit of his loins.

70

"I'm so sorry." She closes the door behind me. I wipe my feet on a pristine jute mat that looks like it's never been used a day in its life. "Luca's flight was delayed. He'll be home any minute, though."

Mellow music plays from speakers—the kind you'd expect someone to play while entertaining the neighbors over platters of expensive meats, aged cheeses, and olives.

Her anxiety is showing.

Straight ahead is some kind of family room with a wall of windows pointing toward the ocean. It's dark now, but I imagine the view is breathtaking—with the kind of price tag that steals the air from your lungs if you're not prepared for it.

A beautiful house for his beautiful wife . . .

I'd heard my husband was doing well for himself, but I didn't realize he was doing *this* well.

All those years I spent sleeping on a dirt floor with a ratty sheet, layers of zip ties digging into the flesh around my ankles, my husband was sleeping safe and sound, living in a cushy lap of luxury in a seaside estate fit for a prince . . .

No one ever said life was fair, but this is downright cruel.

Merritt wanders to the window by the door, rising on her toes and peeking beyond the curtains, one hand on her belly. "Let me just text him and see how far away he is."

"Does he know about me?"

I was hoping I'd be the one to deliver the good news.

Glancing up from her bright screen, she shakes her head. "No. He doesn't."

"So . . . you didn't tell him I was going to be here when he got home?" I feel the need to ask again because the Luca *I* know loathes surprises. One would think being married to him, she'd know that.

Either way, I'm too excited to be upset. In fact, I'm so swollen with anticipation I could burst at my seams.

71

"Ordinarily I wouldn't spring something so heavy on him, but he's got a lot on his plate right now," she says with a tone marinated in sympathy. Does she truly care about him, or is she putting on airs? Time will tell. "I just wanted him to focus on getting home safely."

Her phrasing leads me to think she'd expect him to drive like a bat out of hell to get home if he knew what was waiting for him.

The butterflies in my center work themselves into a nauseating frenzy.

I can't *wait* to see his face when he walks in the door.

Every second until then is torture.

CHAPTER ELEVEN

MERRITT

Luca texts me back within seconds—he's fifteen minutes away.

I feel awful unloading this on him without warning, and I know he isn't the biggest fan of surprises, but selfishly, I want to catch the expression on his face when he sees Lydia again. I want to gauge the gaze in his dark eyes. And I need to hear the first words out of his mouth.

They'll tell me *everything* I need to know.

"Are you hungry?" I gesture toward the kitchen. "I can make you a sandwich?"

I need to make up for the other night, for shutting the door in her face. I don't believe I was in the wrong, given her appearance and the way she showed up on my doorstep so late, but knowing now that she's been through something unspeakable has somewhat softened my reservations.

"I hope turkey's okay . . ." I move first in hopes that she'll follow, and I catch a whiff of my Kilian perfume on the way. It's always tradition to dress up for Luca when he returns from the airport. We usually have a mini date night, something to keep the romance alive and lift our spirits. Tonight will, understandably, be different, but I didn't want to look the way I feel—it would only worry him.

Lydia follows me to the kitchen, her damp sneakers faintly marking the freshly washed hardwood floors from the front door to the marble island.

A moment ago, I was taken aback by her petiteness in our double-height foyer. It visually swallowed her whole. In all my curious wonderings, I'd never once thought about her elfin figure. But I recall, now, the "missing" posters describing her small stature. Five foot one. A hundred pounds. It'd be easy to overpower someone of her meek build—assuming that's what happened.

I know nothing, of course.

Everyone seemed to think she jumped or fell off the cliff that day ten years ago, but the reality is, nobody knows what happened—except her.

"Tomorrow's grocery day," I add as I raid the fridge, grabbing condiments and a dwindling loaf of bread. Wednesdays are typically reserved for household shopping, but with Luca being gone this week, I only made a minirun. Fridays are for date nights. Saturdays are for family outings. Sundays are for lounging. We have a whole system—one that's existed for years. One that's perfect for us. One that may forever cease to exist the second my husband walks in the door tonight.

"Still likes his bread cold, I see." Lydia nods toward the sliced rye wrapped in cellophane, which until a few moments ago, was taking up valuable shelf space next to the butter. Pressing her index finger against her temple, she adds, "I remember these things. It was never just the almonds."

I almost make a joke of it, almost point out all the other things he unnecessarily prefers to keep refrigerated—like peanut butter, potatoes, blackberries, and hot sauce. But I bite my tongue. This isn't an exchange meant for pleasantries. There's nothing cute about this.

This moment is bigger than the two of us. Viscous. Swathed in a million unknowns.

"You can have a seat at the table if you'd like." I work in haste to make her sandwich as the weight of her stare anchors me to the floor. When I'm finished, I wipe my trembling hands on a kitchen towel and deliver her turkey-on-rye with a tight smile.

She doesn't touch it. Not at first. She *studies* it.

Like she doesn't trust it.

I fuss with my hair before sweeping it over one shoulder. "We have mustard. Yellow and Dijon."

I sound like an idiot—and I'm realizing now she didn't even say yes to my offer to make her a sandwich, nor did she confirm she was hungry. But it's too late now. I don't know how to make any of this less awkward. There's nothing natural about marrying a widower, having his children, spending years crafting our dream life—and then answering the door to his dead wife.

All the things I've gleaned about Lydia over the years have been mostly via archived library articles and internet searches. Luca has never liked to talk about her . . . or what happened. It was a painful period in his life, and marrying him meant respecting that. My husband isn't a scab picker or a dweller. Not since he closed the door on his painful history.

Lydia may be his past.

But I'm his present—and forever—wife.

The sandwich dwarfs her hand as her fingertips press into the dark bread. When she finally lifts one corner to her mouth, relief sweeps through me. This is a good sign.

Maybe we *can* make this work? There's a chance this *can* be peaceful and amicable, and we can handle this like the dignified adults that we are.

I fill a glass with seven crescent-shaped ice cubes and retrieve a bottled Fiji water from the fridge, placing both in front of her. She didn't ask for that, either, but it'd be rude not to offer her a beverage.

"I can make you something stronger if you need," I say. "Wine? Vodka?"

Warmth blankets my cheeks as I realize the undercurrent of what I've just said. I might as well have told her she looks worse for the wear. But we both know she's not the edgy one in this situation. Her eyes appear more rested than the last time I saw her. No dark circles this time. Her hair is shorter, too. And a healthy color flushes her complexion. It's truly as though she's come back from the dead.

Our eyes lock as she swallows her bite with a blank expression.

I brace myself in silent hopes that I haven't offended her.

"This is fine. Thank you," she says after an endless pause. Her attention drifts to the icy glass, then back to me.

I remain planted, hesitant to take a seat beside her, because every atom in my body is restless, and having to sit perfectly still in a chair would be torture. Plus, if I keep myself moving, I might be less tempted to fire off a round of preliminary questions before Luca has a chance to ask a single one. It wouldn't be fair to him.

It's been only a few minutes since Lydia arrived, but each second that passes might as well be an hour. Crossing my arms over my chest, I tuck my fingers beneath my arms to keep from fidgeting.

The clock on the microwave reads eleven past eight when Luca's headlights flash through the kitchen window. The garage door opens with a slow, whining grind.

My lips shake, wavy and numb. "He's home."

CHAPTER TWELVE

LYDIA

I shove my dry turkey sandwich aside and follow Merritt's gaze toward a dark hallway off the kitchen. A door opens and closes with a soft click, followed by footsteps on hardwood and the roll of a suitcase. A moment later, a shadowed masculine figure fills the doorway.

"Mer?" he asks when he steps into the light. His thin lips arch into a tender smile when he sees her, and he sniffs out an amused chuckle. Funny—I don't recall ever putting a spark like that in his dark irises. "Why are you just standing there like that?"

"Luca, there's someone here to see you." Merritt's hands are tucked under her arms, and her focus shifts to the island countertop.

He didn't notice me at his kitchen table when he walked in. And why would he? I doubt he's thought of me in a while, and I'm the last person he'd expect to be hanging out with his wife under the comfort of his multimillion-dollar roof.

"Hi, Luca." I rise and keep my tone sweet. "It's been a long time."

His eyes narrow as he takes a step back, and his complexion lightens five shades, as if he's just seen a ghost. Merritt runs a hand across her belly, her attention flicking from our husband to me and back.

"What . . ." His breathy voice fades as he takes a step toward the table. A second later, he braces himself on a chair back, unable to peel his disbelieving scrutiny off me. "How . . . how is this possible?"

"I thought we could all sit down and she could . . . fill us in?" Merritt abandons her perch by the marble island and makes her way over, her pregnant frame occupying the six-foot difference that separates us.

A power move?

A wordless reminder of her place in this equation?

I'm not sure what else to call it.

Luca's jaw slackens as his stare drifts to hers. I'm certain a million scenarios are screaming through his mind—understandably. The dynamic he's come to know and love is shifting in real time, faster than this restaurateur-slash-family-man can keep up with.

"Lydia, why don't you sit back down and get comfortable?" Merritt gestures to my chair. "Luca, settle in. We've got a lot to unpack here."

He says nothing, simply swallowing and sinking into the chair at the head of the table. All that separates us is Merritt and the dead weight of silence lingering in the pine-and-sea-salt-scented air.

"Why don't you start at the beginning—when you went missing?" Merritt suggests with a careful gentleness in her tone.

One would think my husband should be spearheading this conversation, not his expectant wife, who has nothing to do with us, but it seems the proverbial cat has got his tongue.

"All right." I fold my hands until my knuckles whiten, and I home my stare on Luca because he needs to hear every syllable leaving my lips. "It was a typical lazy Sunday . . . Luca had run out to the store to grab a few things, and he was going to gas up the car while he was out. I was sitting around the apartment, bored, I guess. Decided to take a hike while the sun was still out. You'd forgotten your phone, like always." I nod toward my husband. "So I left you a note, telling you I'd gone for a hike and I'd be back soon. Only about an hour in, I stopped by this cliff to catch my breath and take in the sights. Was going to snap a few pictures, too."

I rap my nails on the table, pausing.

Everything that happened after that delineated my wonderfully ordinary "before" from my tragically heinous "after."

The double-wide stainless steel fridge on the other side of the room hums, bringing more life into this room than the chickenshit bastard across from me.

"I was standing there, watching the ocean waves crash on the rocks," I continue, "when a man came up from behind me." My voice trembles, and I stop to swallow the lump that forms in my throat. "He grabbed me, held me tight against him, placed his hand on my mouth, told me to be quiet."

My fingertips tremble and my face grows numb as I attempt to continue. Maybe it's my body reacting to telling my story for the first time . . . all the trauma, all the things it harbored inside for so long are working their way out, like little earthquakes. I force them away as I study my husband's expression, searching for a hint of what he might be thinking in this moment. Only Luca's face is void of any kind of reaction. Poker straight.

But he's listening.

He hasn't stripped his attention away for two seconds.

I'm not even sure he's blinked.

He's got to be shell-shocked. They say mammals have a fight, flight, or freeze response when placed in alarming situations.

Guess Luca's the type to freeze.

"Anyway, he put something over my mouth." Leaning back, I draw in a jagged breath. "A . . . a cloth or something . . . it smelled sort of pungent and sweet." I hover a cupped palm near my lips. "Everything went dark after that."

Merritt leans forward, sliding an elbow on the table and resting her pointed chin on the top of her elegant little hand.

Stoic Luca still hasn't moved a muscle, hasn't made a sound.

"When I woke up, I was strapped to a metal chair in a one-room cabin," I add.

Merritt sucks in a breath, her fingertips tracing her full lips. She's no better than a kid at a campfire listening to a ghost story.

"Then what happened?" Her tone is urgent, impatient.

How rude of me to keep her on the edge of her seat . . .

I direct my attention to my husband. "The man who took me came back."

Merritt adjusts her posture.

"He raped me that first night," I continue, "several times. And he told me—in great detail—all the horrible things he was going to do to me from then on."

Merritt turns to our husband with glassy eyes, but he pays her no mind. His concern is on me—as it should be.

"He was a *sick* man." I wring my hand around the opposite wrist, reminding myself those bindings are no longer there. "Evil incarnate."

"Lydia." Merritt reaches for my hand, but I pull it away.

I didn't come here for her sympathy.

"And for nine years, he tortured me every chance he got in every way you can torture a person," I say through tremoring teeth. Luca's dark eyes strike onto mine. I'm disappointed that he's yet to say a word or show an ounce of emotion, but I know this is a lot to take in without warning. "The Monster—that's what I called him in my head—tried to kill my spirit, my will to live. But he couldn't kill me. And believe me, he tried. Six months ago, he put a cloth sack over my head, marched me out to the forest, and shot me in the back like an old dog."

I leave out the part where I dropped to my knees and pleaded for my life like a goddamned coward. For nine years, all I wanted was for it to end. I'd even prayed for him to put me out of my never-ending misery. But in that moment, with the summer wind skirting across my flesh and birds chirping overhead, I wanted nothing more than a chance to live. To be free.

I swore to him I'd stay away, that I'd never come back, never look for him, never bother him. I promised I'd be as good as dead. And those were my exact words. *As good as dead.*

The Monster's rebuttal came in the form of a gunshot, a white-hot snap against my shoulder blade that knocked me facedown into the earth as the shot echoed through the forest around us.

"Wait," Merritt says, voice tender. "How'd you get away from him?"

I shove my shirt down my left shoulder and angle myself so they can see my back, tracing my fingertips over the raised pink mark where the bullet entered, and then I show them the other side—the exit wound scar.

"I hit the ground as soon as the bullet struck me." I fix my shirt. "And I played dead until he left."

Sometimes at night, when I can't sleep, I still hear the crunch of his boots against fallen leaves and the snap of the twigs beneath his weight. I still taste the broken blades of earth-coated grass in my mouth and the soft graze of a gentle breeze against my face. So much life. So much death. Blood spilled out around me as my adrenaline-fueled heart ricocheted against my chest wall, but I held my breath and lay still—a most impossible task when all I wanted to do was scream until I could no longer feel the blinding-hot sting of the bullet. I must've counted to a thousand before he finally left. And it took me another thousand seconds to muster up the courage to yank the cloth sack off my head and force myself up. An animalistic will to survive took over from there.

The unexpected wail of their daughter's cries cuts through the tension, sending Merritt jolting in her seat and forcing Luca to finally remove his intense gaze from me.

"I've got it," Merritt says, though I didn't see Luca offer.

The moment she disappears, I reach across the table and place my hand over his. My throat squeezes and my stomach roils. I'm hopeful that one day I'll be able to tolerate human touch again.

"I can't tell you how many times I've thought about this moment." I keep my voice low, out of Merritt's earshot. "Seeing you again."

His eyes flash, but he remains statue still.

This must feel dreamlike to him.

I scan the beautiful surroundings of his kitchen, a never-ending expanse of marble and stainless steel, the abundance of fresh flowers and meticulously styled accessories—cutting boards, a butter bell, a vintage recipe tin, copper salt and pepper mills. It's a far cry from our humble beginnings in that run-down one-bedroom apartment on the east side of Bent Creek.

"Looks like you've done pretty well for yourself since I died," I say.

His jaw sets and his temples pulse. "I don't understand . . . why didn't you go to the police after you were shot?"

"Because I wanted to find you first. I wanted you to hear the good news from me—not some small-town sheriff's deputy." Head tilted, I offer a warm smile. "Aren't you happy to see me?"

Sure, I could walk into the Bent Creek police department and speak to a skeptical detective who begrudgingly digs my case file out of an old storage unit. Proving my identity would likely require a DNA test, and those things take time. At that point, word would easily get out that a formerly missing-and-presumed-dead wife of a local businessman is very much alive.

After everything I've been through, I at least deserve to be the bearer of my own good news.

"This is . . . a lot to take in." He forces a hard breath through his nostrils. "Where are you staying?"

"I've been taken in by a woman who runs a shop on the square," I say. "She drove me here tonight, actually. She's helping me get on my feet. Thinks of me like her daughter, in a way. I'd love for you two to meet sometime."

I'm getting ahead of myself. And maybe exaggerating the daughter thing. But I want him to know I'm planting roots and making connections here, because I don't intend to disappear into the night ever again.

"Okay." Merritt returns, kimono billowing and glossy curls springing with each hurried stride. I casually remove my hand from Luca's. She doesn't seem to notice the exchange, or if she does, she pretends not to. "Got Elsie situated. Did I miss anything?"

Did she miss anything? What kind of question is that? This isn't a made-for-TV movie—this is my *life*.

"I was just telling Luca I needed to head out." I retrieve my flip phone from my jacket pocket and text Delphine. It's clear I won't be able to have the conversation I need to have with my husband as long as his wife is around.

Merritt pouts, scanning each of us. Whether she's confused or disappointed, I can't tell, nor do I care. I'm sure she's mourning the details she expected me to entertain her curiosities with tonight.

Luca clears his throat and rises, pushing his chair in but still bracing himself.

"Should we exchange numbers?" Merritt retrieves her phone from a charger by the sink. "I feel like we still need to sort through everything . . ."

"Yeah, good idea," I say, stealing a knowing glance at my husband while his wife isn't looking.

He refuses to return my silent sentiment, instead bearing the look of a man with the weight of the world on his shoulders.

He's got a lot to consider now that I'm back in his life.

Big decisions to make.

Life-changing, even.

A second later, I manage to find my new number on my humble Nokia and prattle it off. Merritt double-checks that she entered the correct one. God forbid she loses her ability to contact me. It's not like I'm going anywhere anyway . . . this is only the beginning.

CHAPTER THIRTEEN

MERRITT

"Where do we go from here?" I ask my pacing husband the second Lydia is gone.

Every time I look at him, all I envision is the controlled captivation in his eyes when he saw her tonight. While he tried to remain unread-able—likely for my benefit—I know him too well. There was something there. A flicker of longing, of wonderment. A piece of him left me in that moment and went straight to her.

Standing in the middle of our bedroom, Luca concentrates on an empty section of carpet by our dresser. I'm not sure he's looked at me for two entire seconds since he walked through the door tonight. His rigid shoulders, stiff posture, and unusual wordlessness paint a portrait of a man bearing the weight of the world.

Kneading the tension from his jaw, he exhales. "I don't know."

He strips out of his clothes, tossing them aside without a second thought. Clearly he's got more important things on his mind. Gripping the side of the bed, I bend to gather his dress shirt from the floor, releas-ing an audible groan.

But he doesn't notice. Or if he does, he doesn't care.

For the bulk of our marriage, he's been a man-with-a-plan. He sees a challenge, he conquers it. If he doesn't have an answer for something, he knows where to find it.

This speechless side of him is concerning.

"What does—" I start to ask another question when he silences me with a lifted palm. I'm not sure he's ever done such a thing before.

I realize this is a lot to dump on this man's plate at once, especially when he's already dealing with the crumbling of his business empire, but I refuse to be muzzled so easily.

"What does this mean for us?" I ask.

Luca stops midstride, his darkened expression intersecting with mine in our lamplit bedroom. Head angled, he exhales.

"Do you even have to ask that?" He uses a tone reserved for unreliable waitstaff, not his loving wife.

But before I respond, everything about him softens, and he closes the space between us, leaning in and brushing his lips against mine in some bizarre pseudo kind of kiss I can only assume is meant to appease me like a silent apology.

"I'm sorry for snapping." He holds me tighter.

I attempt to swallow, but my throat is dry. "What if she's making it up?"

Luca says nothing, merely breathing, existing. He's locked inside that complicated yet beautiful brain of his, which rarely shuts off as it is.

I nestle beneath his arm and rest my cheek against his smooth chest. His heart thunders in my ear.

"Maybe she's . . . ill?" I suggest. "Mentally, I mean. She was so casual about everything . . . a person doesn't go through what she's claiming to have gone through and then speak about it so offhandedly, you know?"

Was she flippant? Or is that what I chose to see? Everything happened so fast, I barely had time to process any of it. And when I left for a few moments to tend to Elsie, who knows what was said, what I missed . . .

All I know is I was gone for maybe a minute or two, and when I came back, she was suddenly in a hurry to leave.

Something had to have been said.

"Did she ask for anything?" I might as well be talking to myself here.

"No," he finally says, his chest rising and falling with one hard breath.

"I didn't tell you this before because I didn't want to worry you when you were out east," I say. "But she stopped by earlier in the week. Just . . . showed up at the door, eight o'clock at night. Told me her name and that she wanted to see you. I told her to leave. And I shut the door in her face. I thought she was some lunatic trying to con us."

He stirs, his body tensing beneath me. "Why didn't you tell me?"

"I had it handled." There's a sternness in my voice, as if I can force him to read between the lines. To remember we're a team. And that we're in this *together*. Always and forever. "I ran into her again in town. Twice, actually. Talked to her a bit. I wanted to be sure it was actually Lydia before I let her anywhere near you."

He pinches the bridge of his nose before rubbing his eyes. "After the week I've had, it would've been nice to know what I was coming home to tonight."

"After the week *you* had?" I inch away from him, my skin growing hot.

Over the course of our relationship, I can count on one hand the number of times my husband has used a condescending tone with me— or withheld sympathy. He's never placed his issues above mine. They've always been side by side, the way an equal partnership should be.

Exhaling, I reexamine this from a different angle.

United we stand, divided we fall is a sentiment that can easily apply to marriages.

"Getting upset with each other isn't going to fix this." I run my palm over his tightening chest, massaging wide circles into his woven muscles in a subtle attempt to calm him. "If I'd have dumped that on you over the phone, you'd have been stressed the whole way home, and you know it. You'd have driven like a maniac and walked in the door all worked up. Forgive me for wanting you home levelheaded and in one piece."

He digests my words before placing his hand on top of mine, a move that somehow feels empty in this moment, like he's simply going through the actions. A second later, he leads me to bed, peeling back the enormous duvet on my side. Is he putting me to bed? Or the issue? I climb in and wait for him to do the same, his feet scuffing against the carpet with an uncharacteristic weight to them.

"What if she's lying?" I ask again. For her sake—and for ours—this would be much easier if it were a lie. "Maybe . . . maybe she ran away all those years ago for whatever crazy reason she had at the time . . . and then came back with this story because she thinks it'd make us feel sorry for her and maybe we'd give her money or something? I saw the way she looked around our house . . ."

He sits in contemplative silence, though we both know it's a stretch.

"It's strange that she hasn't gone to the police, you know?" I continue. "After everything she's claiming, a person would think that's the first place she'd run to."

Luca exhales. "Regardless of what did or didn't happen, I don't think she's in a good state of mind. We need to be careful. *You* need to be careful. There's something off about her . . ."

"Is there a chance it isn't Lydia?"

"It's her," he says without pause.

My heart plummets, overpowering any shred of hope I had left. I breathe him in, close my eyes, and hold myself in the fleeting present for a moment until our unborn son stirs inside me. I place Luca's hand on my belly out of habit. Fullness floods my body—the manifestation of assurance, perhaps, or a reminder that as long as we're together, everything's going to be okay.

Miracles happen all the time. This baby is proof of that.

"Promise you'll stay away from her." Luca's tone is stern, uncompromising, and he removes his hand from my stomach. "Whatever she's been through, it's changed her. If she comes around again—and I imagine she will—let me deal with her."

This is the man I know—fiercely protective, unquestionably loyal.

I never should have doubted him . . . he just needed a moment to process everything.

"You don't think she'd do something to *us* . . . do you?" My voice breaks as the reality of those words washes through me. She can do whatever she wants to me, but if she so much as thinks about laying a hand on my children—I'll do whatever I have to do, and I'll sleep like a baby afterward.

"I'm sure it bothers her to see that I've moved on . . . and that I'm happy."

I thread my fingers through his and try to imagine this from Lydia's perspective. Whether she's in a rational state of mind or not, it has to be frustrating seeing how Luca has moved on and flourished after her disappearance. Life has been kinder to him than it's ever been to her. That has to be difficult to accept.

"So what do we do now?" I ask.

"*We* do nothing." He leans in to kiss my forehead. "This is my problem, not yours."

With those words, he puts the conversation to bed, and I close my eyes, listening and waiting for him to fall asleep himself.

But he never does.

And for the eight hours that follow, we lie in bed—a married couple pretending to sleep, pretending our life isn't falling apart or changing in ways we never could've anticipated. Feigning, in deafening silence, that everything is going to be perfectly fine come what may.

When the sun rises outside our picture window, I creep out of bed and tiptoe downstairs to make his coffee and slice some fruit for breakfast. Chopping bananas and strawberries, I make a list of silent promises to myself: to trust my husband, to stand by him no matter what, and to do whatever it takes to keep this family together—because I can't shake the feeling that Lydia wants nothing more than to see us fall apart.

And to be honest, if our roles were reversed and I were her—I'd want the same.

CHAPTER FOURTEEN

LYDIA

"Your friend from last night," Delphine says over coffee Sunday morning. "I forgot to ask his name?"

"Luca Coletto."

Her lips tighten at one side. "Name sounds vaguely familiar . . . you'd think after three years of living here, I'd know more of the locals by now."

"He owns a few restaurants in town." I take another sip. "Coletto's by the Sea is the big one."

I was trekking along the Oregon coast last month when I stopped into a middle-of-nowhere café for a coffee and shelter from the rain. A couple of retirement-aged men came in behind me, and the hostess seated them in the booth to my right. For the hour that followed, I listened to them ramble on about their nagging wives who are "never in the mood these days," their dream cars—a Shelby Cobra and a '57 Chevy, respectively—and their latest business endeavors. Apparently they were partners, moderately successful venture capitalists with their ears to the ground.

I tuned them out for the most part . . . until they started talking about some guy by the name of Luca Coletto who owned a slew of restaurants in "some tourist town" called Bent Creek.

With pricked ears and hands wrapped casually around a ceramic mug, I feasted on their gossip since they were obviously speaking of *my* Luca Coletto.

And thank God I did.

Because then they began blathering about how he was some overnight millionaire restaurateur with a handful of concept restaurants, a mansion by the ocean, and a "smoking hot" wife. Avoiding eye contact, I listened for entertainment purposes, absorbing every last fact, figure, and tidbit of conjecture. But after a few minutes, I couldn't take it any longer. Tossing a handful of change on the table, I grabbed my backpack and got the hell out of there.

While I was sleeping on dirt floors and enduring weekly rapes, my husband was living the dolce vita. All those times I'd wondered what his life was like without me, I'd never imagined him with a beautiful wife or the amount of success that has strangers gossiping dozens of miles away.

And after everything that had happened, I never expected him to stick around Bent Creek.

Three hours later, I was already in the next town over. A woman on a mission. I hiked—and at times, hitchhiked—over the course of several weeks. And when I arrived at the town I once shared with my former beloved, I asked anyone who'd give me the time of day where I could find the Coletto residence. I got lucky when I stumbled upon a jaded former employee working at a Chevron. He told me exactly where I could find Luca, no questions asked.

I sip my coffee at Delphine's kitchen table, hiding a barely there simper behind my floral mug as I envision the next leg of my journey to settle the score with this pathetic excuse for a life.

My thoughts drift to Merritt. Less than two seconds around her, and I can tell she's an anxious type. Shallow too. Or maybe it's introversion with a generous side of dull personality. She's not exactly charismatic. Hardly magnetic. I get the sense she *looks* more interesting than she is, buzzing around in her fancy car with her expensive hair and curated wardrobe. She's a human accessory.

The pity practically radiated off her in atomic-sized waves last night.

I'm willing to bet she feels sorry for me. And she should. I hope her heartstrings are pulled so taut they're on the verge of snapping.

I finish my coffee, wash and dry the mug, and tell Delphine I'm going for a walk.

Stepping into the fresh air, I know one thing for sure—today is the first day of the rest of my *new* life.

CHAPTER FIFTEEN

MERRITT

"You made such a mess, sweet pea. Look at your face, silly girl." I'm cleaning up after Elsie's lunch when it hits me . . .

We should help Lydia.

It's the only way out of this mess.

If we get her on her feet, get her settled somewhere—preferably far from Bent Creek—if we help her start a new life and ensure she's comfortable . . . maybe she'll move on and leave us be?

I lift Elsie over the sink, helping her wash her hands, though she just wants to play in the bubbles. Outside, a sedan motors past. Nothing that I recognize. But for a second, a piece of me hoped it was Luca coming home early from work.

We spent the entirety of Sunday pretending nothing was wrong. He played with Elsie. I read a parenting book and made lists of prospective baby names. It was strange—but also therapeutic—to pretend everything was fine.

We even made love last night, which I took as his way of letting me know where I stand in this unprecedented hierarchy.

This morning, Luca woke early, jogged three miles on the treadmill, hit the shower, and kissed me goodbye on his way to work. And he was in such a hurry, he forgot the travel mug of coffee I'd prepared for him.

Hoisting Elsie on my hip, I take her to the family room and place her in the center of the room before gathering books and toys to keep her busy. While she plays, I chew the corner of my lip, running mental math as I try to figure out what it would take to get Lydia on her feet. We could probably find her a used car for a few grand. Maybe buy her a little house in some small town in the Midwest where real estate is cheaper than dirt. Fifty thousand? Seventy-five? Maybe twenty grand for a trade degree or some training, something to secure a career for her.

I'm 99 percent sure we don't have an extra hundred grand lying around, so we'd have to borrow against our 401(k) . . . again.

Luca's not going to like that idea, but if it means getting Lydia out of our hair and feeling like we've done a bit of good for her, maybe he'll warm up to it?

All I know is this must be extremely difficult for her . . . Anything we can do to blunt that edge will benefit us all in the end.

I sneak off to pluck my phone from the charger in the kitchen, and when I return, I tap out a message to Lydia, asking if she'd like to spend some one-on-one time together today, and then I hit send.

She writes back seven minutes later with a simple I'd love that.

Interesting choice of words from someone who has every right to resent my existence.

Settling back into the cushions, I watch my daughter play, grateful that she's blissfully unaware of the maelstrom brewing around her. If all goes as planned, she'll never know.

The storm will pass, and it'll be like it never happened at all.

CHAPTER SIXTEEN

LYDIA

"Everyone should have a signature scent." Merritt plucks a tester from a frilly pink display at some boutique in the shopping district. Spraying a white strip of paper, she fans it a few times before offering it to me. "What do you think of this one?"

Look at us.

Just a couple of Bent Creek wives shopping on a weekday afternoon.

I lift the cardstock paper to my nose and inhale. It smells like cherry blossoms and vanilla, an overpowering smack in the face disguised in a frosted, hourglass-shaped bottle.

I must have made a face because Merritt laughs. "Too strong?"

She grabs another, this one in an emerald-green bottle, the label calling it SWEET ELIXIR. It makes me think of Delphine. I thought I was her pet project, but evidently I'm Merritt's, too. The instant I climbed into her purring Beamer this morning, she handed me an iced latte and told me she's taking me shopping. Her treat.

Which we both know is actually Luca's treat, because she does nothing but prance around their mansion-by-the-sea like some wannabe SoCal housewife while he brings home the bacon.

"What about this one?" Merritt moves to another counter and selects a pink Lancôme bottle. I don't have to smell it to know I'll like it. Back in high school, it's what all the girls wore. Every hallway smelled like this musky magnolia-jasmine concoction. The closest I ever came to wearing it was rubbing a magazine sample against my wrists when I happened to come across an ad.

I lift the bottle to my nose, not wasting time with the testing strips, and inhale.

"You're smiling," she says, voice singsong. "You like?"

I nod. I *do* like. And it just so happens I like it so much I'm willing to overlook the fact that this entire moment is so removed from reality it's laughable. If Merritt truly believes lavishing me with little luxuries is going to change the inevitable, she's not only delusional, she's a damned fool.

I clear any remnants of superficial glee from my lips.

"Then there it is." She claps her slender hands together, feet firmly planted in her alternate reality. "You officially have a signature scent."

An employee in a white vest saunters up to us, and Merritt wastes no time telling her she'd like a three-ounce bottle of the eau de parfum.

"You don't have to do this," I say—after she slides her glossy black credit card across the counter and the woman carries it off to the register.

Merritt waves it away, brows knitting. "Don't be silly. This is my treat. After everything you've been through—and what you came home to—you have my full sympathies. I just want to help you any way I can. Figured a little shopping and a light lunch might help us get to know each other better, too. Our situation is . . . *unique*. But I know we can navigate it together."

If I didn't know better, I'd think she's attempting to buy my friendship. Or my loyalty. Or my sympathy. Something. She's definitely buying more than a fragrance. And it's sad, if I think about it too much—the fact that her only power is wielded from a tiny plastic rectangle.

The associate returns with my perfume wrapped in a pink bag and secured with a white satin ribbon. She hands it to Merritt first, who shakes her head and points to me. The woman's sweet expression sours when she takes me in—and I can't blame her. I don't have the radiant glow of a woman who gets bimonthly facials. My hair is thin and lifeless, the cut crooked (bless Delphine's heart). There isn't a speck of makeup on my face. And I'm wearing another one of Amber's outfits, which I deduced are at least fifteen years past their prime after finding a pair of black gaucho pants in the mix this morning. I was tempted to wear them for sheer comfort, but I opted for some low-slung flare jeans and a burgundy velour hoodie with a *J* on the zipper and *Juicy* spelled out across the back.

"Should we check out shoes next?" Merritt points to the back of the shop, where five wall racks display an assortment of footwear—most of them suited for cooler weather. None of them as practical as tennis shoes.

She waddles—albeit elegantly, if that's possible—to the shoe area, browsing for a second before selecting a pair of black leather boots. In any other store, I'd assume they were meant for hiking. But here I get the impression these are meant to be a fashion statement.

"Maybe something more every day?" I reach for a canvas TOMS shoe in a shade of bleeding-heart red. While the color won't go with much, they'll stay cleaner than these white Keds I found in the donation bin of a shelter five towns over.

Her manicured brows rise as she inspects them without touching. And then she offers a polite, "Mm-hmm. Yeah. Those could be nice."

She doesn't like them.

Ordinarily it wouldn't matter if she didn't like them, but she's the one throwing down the plastic.

"I'm just a tennis shoes kinda girl." I try to lighten the tone and add a shoulder shrug. "Boots are great, they can just get kind of heavy for every day."

"But do you like them?" She holds up the black boot, and I catch a glimpse of the $200 price tag dangling from the tongue.

"Yeah, they're nice." I mentally calculate how many TOMS a girl could buy with two hundred bucks while I pretend the price doesn't floor me.

"Why don't we do both?" She takes the canvas shoe from my hand and raises it over her head, flagging the attention of a bored-looking associate by the register. "Could we try these on?"

"Size six," I say.

"In a size six," she calls over the chill music pumping through the speakers.

The associate nods, disappearing into a back room and returning with two boxes stuffed with tissue paper and pantyhose socks. I take a seat and try them on while Merritt watches.

"Walk around and make sure they're comfortable." She points, watching me. Such a *mom*. Not that I know what that's like. My mom was always bringing home hand-me-downs from various coworkers when I was younger. I'm not sure we ever set foot in an actual store together. "They good? Think they'll work?"

I slide the second pair off and set them carefully in the box. "Are you sure you want to get these? You just bought me perfume . . ."

"Lydia." She splays a hand across her décolletage, over the diamond pendant hanging down to her cleavage. Eyes glistening, she says, "It would be an honor and a privilege to help you get back on your feet."

I can't do emotions. Or emotional people. I had to tamp that shit down early on, or The Monster would feed off it. It was chum to a shark. I didn't want to give him more than I had to.

"Stop. Come on. Don't cry." I wave my hand, frantic, as if it could make the tears dissipate before they have a chance to slide down her creamy pink cheeks and ruin her flawless makeup. If we were true friends, maybe I'd hug her—or at the very least, rub her arm out of comfort. "There's nothing sad about this. This is awesome. I love these shoes. Love the perfume. And I'm enjoying my time with you."

I add the last line as a bonus, figuring a little white lie won't hurt her. If things were different, maybe I would enjoy my time with her. Guess we'll never know.

Within seconds, she fans her eyes, manages a laugh, and composes herself. This can't be easy for her—my return to Luca's life. I don't want to make this harder for her than it already is. None of this is her fault.

"What about a coat? Do you need a winter coat? I know you have a light jacket, but it gets cold out here sometimes . . ." She switches gears, scanning the various racks of jeans, tops, and sweaters until she settles on a small selection of seasonal gear. Puffy coats, mostly. The kind meant to make you look like an expensive marshmallow on the ski slopes.

But I *do* need a coat.

While I'd prefer not to look like the Michelin Man, beggars can't be choosers and all that jazz.

We find an extrasmall in "snowcap white." The last one on the rack in my size. I drape it over my arm and give it a squeeze because I can't resist. The tag on the sleeve reads $349. With the shoes and the perfume, we're already well over six hundred bucks, and she's started eyeing the sweater section.

"Tops? How are you doing on sweaters? Do you need blouses? Anything like that?" Merritt asks next, making her way to a new section.

"You *really* don't have to do this." I follow.

She offers a polite smile, obligatory almost. And her focus is soft—until it settles on the dangling *J* on my zipper. She couldn't hide the undercurrent of revulsion if she tried.

I'm sure I look ridiculous in my velour getup, like I just stepped out of a September 2006 issue of *Us Weekly*. But I've got no one to impress, and I don't want to offend Delphine by replacing her dead daughter's clothes with fancy new threads. At least not all at once. It should be a gradual process, much like mourning and moving on. Little by little. One step at a time.

"I think we're good for today, don't you?" I make one final visual sweep of the chic boutique surroundings, knowing full well I don't belong here.

She scans the store one more time as well, lingering on the jeans section before she sighs.

"Yeah. You're right," she says, hand gliding across her smooth bump. "We can always come back another time. Are you hungry? I'm famished."

My body learned long ago how to shut off those hunger signals. It's like a broken stoplight constantly flashing red. I'm rarely hungry. Most foods irritate my stomach anyway, and more often than not, I forget to eat until I'm hit with a screaming headache.

"Yeah. Starving," I say because I'm not about to walk off with this massive haul and turn down her invitation. There may be a multitude of questionable things in my DNA, but rudeness isn't one of them. "What's good around here?"

We carry our items to the register, laying everything across the glass counter.

"We own a deli just a few doors down," she says. "Monday's clam chowder day, and believe me when I say we have the best clam chowder on the entire Oregon coast."

I lift my brows and pretend to be blown away by that fact.

I've never had clam chowder in my life.

"All right. Sold. Let's do it," I say.

We finish the transaction with the swipe of her black credit card and carry our bags to the deli on the corner.

"Mrs. Coletto," a red-haired teenager says in greeting. Despite it being nearly noon, the place is dead. Just a man in a gray suit finishing lunch in the back. Other than that, it's just the two of us. "How's the boss man? Haven't seen him in a while."

"Busy as ever." She offers him a breathy smile, then points to the menu and leans closer to me. "The soups are there, on that first panel.

Highly recommend the chowder, though. In the second column are the salads. Then there are wraps. They can make anything you want, and it's all amazing. Can't go wrong with any of it."

Overwhelmed by choices, I find myself momentarily distracted by the crystal chandeliers hanging above the register. The crisp white walls, outfitted in vintage photography art in mismatched frames, also seem like an unneeded touch. This is, after all, a glorified sub shop, is it not?

We order our meals, grab our numbers (gold leafed, I might add), and find a table in the back corner, sidling up in chairs fit for a French bistro.

"Thank you so much for lunch," I say. "And for . . . everything. I have to admit, when you said you wanted to get together, this wasn't what I was expecting."

She rests a casual elbow on the table, head tilted as she examines me, wide smile covering her pretty face. "I just want to do what I can to make this an easy transition . . . for everyone."

Is that all she's trying to do? Or is she afraid I've come back to steal my husband out from under her? It's hard to tell. I'm still trying to figure this one out. Sometimes I look at her and see this vapid, flittering, insecure housewife, and other times I swear I catch a deepness in her cool crystalline eyes, something hidden inside an unreadable expression or two.

"So how did you meet Luca?" she asks when our drinks arrive. She glides a paper straw into her sparkling ice water and slides the glass closer.

"We worked together at a little diner," I say. "Back in Greenbrook, Washington."

"Ah, that's right. He told me that once. I remember now." She titters, her frost-white teeth contrasting against her glossy pink-nude lips. I don't believe for one second this woman hasn't googled me or asked her husband all the right questions. She'd have to be certifiable not to be curious about her predecessor, especially given the circumstances.

"What about you?" I flip it around.

"We met shortly after I moved out west. I'm actually from Maryland." She sits straighter, proper almost. Well-bred good girl mode. "My parents lived there all their lives. They had me . . . then nine years later they had my sister. It was an interesting upbringing, I guess you could say. Adair and I each attended boarding school from second grade on. We came home for summers and holidays. Our family wasn't what you'd call close. Not by any stretch of the imagination. Sometimes I wonder if I'm overcompensating with Luca and Elsie . . ."

That didn't answer my question . . .

"So what brought you here?" I ask, hoping for a bread crumb or two that might help me understand how she and Luca came to be, because the Luca I knew was far from debutante husband material.

"Rebellion, I suppose." There's a glint in her soft irises. "Fell in love with an art school I found online. It was unaccredited but fabulous, staffed with world-renowned artists. It was more of an apprenticeship arrangement than a formal education. My father would've preferred that I'd followed in his footsteps and attended Brown. But something in my heart just told me to come here." She shrugs. "So I did . . . and I've never left."

"Do they visit?"

Her shoulders drop as she sips her water. "There was a falling-out shortly after I came here. Um, money related mostly. My mother passed unexpectedly my senior year of high school, and my father wasted no time remarrying the most dreadful woman. And because I wasn't attending Brown—or any other school he could brag to his country club friends about—he told me I was on my own." Merritt exhales, her posture righting once more. "He's never set foot on Oregon soil. Hasn't met Luca—only seen him in the Christmas cards we send each year. No interest in meeting his grandchild. And I'm not sure there'll ever be . . . he has a new family now—he and his latest wife just adopted three little ones from some Russian orphanage. Honestly, I couldn't even tell you their names." She lifts a finger. "Not that I'm proud of that fact."

Pressing my lips, I offer sympathy. I know how complicated child and parent relationships can be. I could probably write an expert-level thesis on the topic, sell it to some desperate grad student on the black market, and land them a solid A.

"I'm sorry," I say, "about losing your mom."

"Thank you. I miss her every day." Her eyes glisten with the threat of tears, but she smiles until it disappears. "I know she'd be proud, seeing what I've become. And I just know she'd adore Luca and Elsie."

"Table eleven." A staff member takes our gold-plated numbers and delivers our soups in thick white bowls with tiny pearl accents on the rim—again not meant for a deli in my humble opinion. This entire place looks like a spoiled wife's pet project sponsored by a love-drunk husband who green-lit it all.

"Bon appétit." Merritt digs her spoon into her chowder, watching me take my first bite. I taste salt, cream, smoky bacon, and a hint of ocean water. I've eaten worse. "So? Verdict?"

Despite growing up on the coast, I've never been a lover of seafood. It was never something we ate at home since it wasn't exactly a budget-friendly grocery item. The closest I ever got was the occasional fish sandwich blue plate special at the diner, but I'm convinced you could fry me a sock and it would taste amazing.

"Divine." I close my eyes and force myself to savor the off-white mush. "You weren't kidding."

She sinks back in her seat, exhaling as if she's relieved—as if my opinion matters.

For all my imperfections and shortcomings, I thank my lucky stars insecurity was never one of them.

"So how long do you think you'll stay in Bent Creek?" Merritt asks after our wraps arrive. Her inflection is casually inquisitive, but I can spot a loaded question a mile away.

Fortunately I'm one step ahead of her.

"Not sure," I say. "Taking things one day at a time."

She dabs the down-turned corners of her mouth with a napkin, chewing, contemplating. I can imagine she's deeply unsatisfied with my ambiguity.

"The man who did those horrible things to you." She pauses. "Do you know who he is? Where he is? Are you worried he's going to come after you?"

I rest my spoon aside and straighten the napkin in my lap. "So much for casual conversation . . ."

"I'm sorry . . . I won't pretend to understand what you went through," she says, keeping her voice low, "but I can only imagine how difficult it must have been to come back and to see your husband with a brand-new life. And I keep trying to put myself in your shoes. Your head must be spinning. It must be exhausting trying to figure out your next step."

Her diamond ring—a massive pear shape surrounded with hundreds of tiny diamonds—glints in the midday sun, throwing specks of light on the wall beside us.

"I'm sure it isn't easy for you to sit here and pretend like none of this is . . . weird," she continues. "There's no precedent for this sort of thing. No manual. I appreciate that you're so open and willing to take things one day at a time." Her lips teeter into a nervous chuckle. "You just . . . You hear all these horror stories and read all these articles about people doing horrible things to one another over *men* . . ." Her voice trails, and she emphasizes *men* as if it's a silly little word that means nothing to her when we both know the truth. "All of this is to say—I'm just glad that isn't us."

This is the equivalent of a dog showing its belly, submitting to another dog, attempting to show it's harmless and doesn't want to fight.

Of course, she doesn't want things to get ugly—she's from good stock. She was probably raised to bury her problems under a mountain of cash and drink top-shelf vodka until any and all emotional pain subsides, but seeing how she's pregnant and fully dependent on her husband to support her easy lifestyle, I imagine she's feeling extraordinarily vulnerable these days.

"I'll admit it stings," I say. "Seeing Luca and you, so happy, so perfect. You've created this picture-perfect dream life together. And I can tell you love him."

Though I can't tell if he loves her. The other night, he didn't give her more than a passing glance after he saw me.

She lifts a hand to her heart, her diamonds throwing even more dancing lights on the wall.

"He's a *good* man," she says.

I offer a bittersweet smile. "The best. I'm just glad he was able to move past everything so easily." I reach for my water. "Losing a spouse the way he did . . . you'd think it'd stick with a person."

"I'm not sure he moved on from everything so much as he accepted that he couldn't change the past." She sips her drink, the straw taut between her thumb and forefinger. "If I'm being honest, I was the one who finally convinced him it was okay to marry again."

She rests her glass on the table, face contorting as if she's got more to say—only she must have second thoughts because she reaches for her wrap instead, adding nothing.

I clear my throat. "Can I ask you something?"

"Anything." She dabs her mouth and leans in like she's living for this conversation.

"What did you see in Luca when you first met him? What made you think he's the one?" Not that her answer matters. Simply filling in blanks here.

Lashes fluttering and her mouthful of teeth on full display, she exudes radiance. "Oh, gosh. Where do I start?"

The Luca I first met over a decade ago had overgrown hair in constant need of a wash, a trim, or both. He was average in build and height, introverted, never one to dominate a conversation or command a room. The kind of guy you pass at the grocery store and mentally categorize as a background prop, like an extra in a movie scene.

The two of us together, average and ordinary, never made anyone look twice, and that was part of the reason we were so perfect together.

The woman before me with her New England upbringing and old-moneyed breeding, with her style and good taste . . . what could she have possibly seen in someone like that?

"He was different," she begins. "Different from everyone else, I mean. He was mysterious without being closed off. Loyal without being possessive. Well read without being pretentious about it. And he was good with his hands—he could fix just about anything, electrical, mechanical, you name it. He wasn't like the guys back home or any of the guys I grew up around." She stirs her drink with her straw, elbow on the table, and exhales as she concentrates on something in the distance, a lovestruck half smile forming on her perfect pout. "I saw him, and I just knew . . . he was perfect for me."

I place the mental image of Luca-from-ten-years-ago next to the beautiful, glowing woman across from me, and it simply won't compute. Perhaps she saw something special in him, something that couldn't be seen with the naked eye.

"How did you two meet, anyway?" I pick at my food, my stomach growing unsettled as it tends to when I eat anything rich anymore.

"We were neighbors," she says. "Both renting out opposite halves of a little duplex over on Acadia Drive. He fixed my fridge one night, and I invited him to stay for a glass of wine . . . which turned into a few glasses." She chuckled. "We talked all night, until the sun came up. Now here we are."

Merritt rubs her belly, blowing a hard breath from pursed lips.

"You okay?"

She nods. "Braxton-Hicks contractions—it's normal this late in the game."

"When are you due?"

"Soon." It's her turn to be vague.

"Oh, so this spring?" I call her bluff. We're six weeks from the official first day of spring, and while I don't know much about pregnancies, I know when a woman looks like she's two seconds from bursting at the seams.

She chuckles. "Early March."

Still no date, but close enough.

I imagine she doesn't trust me. Perhaps she's seen one too many Lifetime movies and thinks I'm here to rip her baby straight from the womb and run off with it.

"Do you know what you're having?" I ask next.

Merritt sips her water. "A boy."

"How perfect. A girl and a boy," I say. "Luca must be thrilled."

"He's excited." She beams again, as if someone flipped a switch to power her back on. God, pregnancy looks exhausting. I can't imagine running an entire gamut of emotions on a daily basis and still being able to put myself together and go shopping with my husband's undead wife. "This little guy was a total surprise."

"What's Luca like?" I ask. "As a father I mean."

"Wonderful." Her gaze grows unfocused, as if she's lost in thought. "Doting and gentle and attentive. More patient than most. Protective."

Merritt's hand splays across her rotund middle for the millionth time today. Eyes squeezed tight, she winces.

"You sure you're okay?" I ask.

Zoned out, she breathes in through her nose and out through her mouth a few times before finally nodding. "That one was a little more intense than the others. I hate to call it a day, but I think I probably should go home and lie down while I still have the nanny."

Nanny? She has a nanny?

She has one kid and no job . . .

"Of course." I fold my napkin and drape it across my plate.

We gather our things and head out to her olive-green SUV with its space-age headlights. Climbing into the warm, buttery leather seats, I inhale the scent of new car and paper shopping bags and try to imagine what kind of life she'd lead if all this went away.

I imagine Merritt with two tantrummy children in a two-bedroom apartment on the square. A pile of bills rests on the kitchen counter next to spilled Cheerios and a store-brand apple juice box. Their furniture—much of it left over from their seaside estate—a jarring contrast against the gray plaster walls, grimy carpet, and almond-colored appliances.

"This might come across as strange," Merritt says when she pulls up to The Blessed Alchemist a few minutes later. "But how would you feel about spending more time with us? As a family?"

Unbuckling, I stifle a scoff and turn to her. "What are you proposing?"

Does she honestly think we could be one big, happy modern family?

"I think if we all spent a little more time together, got to know each other better, things might feel less . . . surreal?" She shrugs. "And maybe we'd each get the closure we need?"

I don't need closure—I need my life back. The one I was always meant to have.

"I'm not sure what you mean by *we'd each get closure*," I say. "Do *you* need closure?"

She hesitates, tripping over her words. "I'm not trying to make this about me . . . I'm just thinking of Luca. And you, of course. There's no guidebook on this kind of thing, you know? But we could figure this out together. One day at a time."

I offer a dramatic pause, leaning against the headrest and staring straight ahead as if I'm contemplating my answer—like I don't already know damn well what I'm going to say.

"You know, that's not a bad idea," I finally respond.

She exhales, like she'd been holding her breath that whole time. "Wonderful. I'll text you tomorrow."

"I'll be waiting." I grab my bags from the back seat and head into Delphine's shop. Fortunately she's with a customer, too preoccupied to notice the giant shit-eating grin covering my face.

Merritt's IQ has to be akin to the department store lipstick she keeps in her designer satchel . . . because this is almost too easy.

CHAPTER SEVENTEEN

"Rough day?" I ask when Luca pours himself two fingers of Scotch after work.

I can't remember the last time I saw him drink at home. He's never been a fan of alcohol, typically ordering a cocktail or beer at dinners out mostly for show. The minibar we installed during the remodel was predominantly for me. When not with child, I enjoy a nice glass of cabernet with dinner or the occasional top-shelf cocktail on the weekends. The Scotch was a Christmas gift from several years ago. The $200 collector's bottle imported from Scotland went perfectly with the Baccarat crystal tumblers I'd bought us for our first wedding anniversary. They were the perfect complements to our well-appointed home bar. But this is perhaps the third time I've ever seen my husband so much as go near that bottle.

I'm hopelessly wild about Luca, but not when he's drunk. There's a darkness in his eyes when he overindulges. He slurs and rambles and becomes testy. Wine doesn't affect him as much as the hard stuff, but he generally avoids both.

He tosses the entire thing back in one gulp, wearing a pained expression when he's finished. My esophagus burns with phantom sympathy.

I'll have to keep an eye on him.

"Come." I thread my fingers through his. The roast chicken I put in the oven still has another ten minutes. "Let's sit down and relax for a bit . . ."

I lead him to the family room, where Elsie plays with her little dollhouse and the wooden family I had specially made from some local artisan in Bent Creek. Little wooden versions of Luca, Elsie, me, and the baby.

We sink into the sofa cushions together, and I nuzzle up to him, inhaling the cocktail of restaurant scents that cling to his dress shirt.

"Heard anything from out east?" I ask. Out of three pitches, there has to be someone.

"One said definitely not." His body tenses with his words. "The other said they were waiting until next week, after a shareholder meeting. Nothing from the third."

"I'm not worried." It's a little white lie. I don't tend to make a habit out of dishonesty, but someone needs to be the beacon of hope.

"That makes one of us." He stares out the picture window, toward the gray seascape beyond our backyard. It isn't like him to be so gloom and doom, but I don't hold it against him. His mind must be laden with worry and doubt and uncertainty.

"I, um, had lunch with Lydia today," I say. But before he allows me to explain, he flies off the sofa and grabs a fistful of his dark hair.

"Jesus Christ, Merritt." His dark eyes burn with a fiery haze. "What the hell are you thinking? She's not your friend. Did I or did I not tell you to stay away from her?"

I stay calm—mostly for Elsie's sake and for the baby, but also because Luca needs to simmer, and meeting his frenzy with mine won't help anything.

"I just think . . . if we could help her get on her feet," I say, rising, confident. "I think that's all she wants—all she needs."

His arms fold, muscles straining against the white fabric of his button-down.

"Luca, the woman had holes in her shoes. She literally has nothing," I say, keeping my tone as casual as if we were discussing tomorrow's dinner menu.

"So, what . . . you're going to buy her a new wardrobe and send her on her way? Is that how you think this is going to pan out?"

"I don't know how it's going to pan out," I say. "But I think taking a rational approach to this, handling it like grown adults, being generous in whatever ways we can—"

"Generous?" He tugs a handful of hair again. "Generous, Merritt? I just laid off three servers today. And tomorrow, I'm shuttering the coffee shop. That's eight more out of jobs. We can't afford to be generous, and even if we could . . . you need to run these things by me."

The timer on the oven chimes. I meet his wild regard with one of my own. "I'm only trying to help."

"Daddy!" Elsie runs to her father, arms outstretched. He scoops her up, kissing her cheek as his stare locks on mine.

For the first time in remembrance, I can't begin to know what he's thinking.

He turns his attention to our daughter, and I toddle to the kitchen, my belly sore from a day of Braxton-Hicks. While I'm well aware of our financial situation and it pains me to hear of the layoffs, I will not be treated like an imbecile.

I'm going to right this ship—with or without his permission.

CHAPTER EIGHTEEN

LYDIA

"Just one today?" The doll-faced strawberry blonde hostess with lashes up to her eyebrows and a whittled waist greets me at Coletto's by the Sea.

I nod, scanning the dreamy restaurant bathed in natural light.

Grabbing a linen menu, she leads me to a corner table for two flanked with windows and a perfect view of the crashing waters. A tea light candle glimmers next to wooden salt and pepper mills, and piano music mixes with tinkling silverware to create a relaxing ambience. Overhead, exposed wood beams complete the experience, adding an earthy, homegrown touch.

Poring over the menu, I laugh out loud at the prices. Literally.

Twenty-five dollars for a bowl of oyster soup?

One-fifty for sea bass?

A thirty-dollar house salad?

Either Luca's a brilliant businessman—or success has made him greedy.

"Hi, I'm Jolie, and I'll be your server today." A twentysomething girl with a mess of caramel curls piled on top of her head brings me a glass of iceless water. "Can I start you out with something from our drink menu? We're featuring our Walnut Grove Malbec today, or I can bring you a list of our cocktail specials."

"Iced tea. Please," I say. "Thank you."

Having worked in the serving industry before, I've learned that the kindest patrons are the ones who say "please" and "thank you" right off the bat. It sets a precedent. And it's a sign of respect, basic human decency. It almost always guarantees you decent service.

"I'll be right back with that."

I study the menu in her absence. Since I'm not hungry, nothing jumps out. Delphine had the random urge to whip up a big breakfast this morning, and like a pampered bohemian queen, I feasted off egg white spinach omelets and ancient grain toast with local strawberry jam. Better than anything on this pretentious menu.

Regardless, I didn't come here to eat.

I locate the most expensive item—a surf and turf special featuring a filet mignon and fresh Maine lobster, which the menu boasts is imported daily.

Two hundred bucks.

With prices like this, no wonder he's doing so well for himself.

I have her throw the house salad in as well. And a chocolate soufflé for dessert because the menu states they require a thirty-minute lead time.

A few minutes later, my order is taken and I'm left all to my lonesome. The couple at the table beside me hold hands, staring deep into one another's eyes in a nausea-inducing display of young love. Across from them is a group of middle-aged women with oversized diamonds, carefree laughs, and colorful cocktails. To the far left is a segmented area set up like a party room, and two staff are setting the table with meticulous detail while one is posting a RESERVED FOR THE BEAUMONT PARTY sign.

Jolie returns with my house salad—a soggy, weedy mix strewn with shaved parmesan. I've seen bowls of ranch-drenched iceberg presented better than this.

"Can I get you anything else, miss?" Jolie asks, hands clasped behind her back.

"Yes, actually." I lean in. "Could you send Luca Coletto over here?"

A flash of panic colors her face, but I intervene.

"I'm an old friend of his." I offer a well-meaning smile. "I saw his car outside, just wanted to say hello."

At least I assume the blinding-white Maserati coupe with LCOLE86 on the plate is his . . .

"Of course." Her expression softens as she strolls to the back of the restaurant and disappears down a hallway.

I stab the kale and dandelion greens with my fork before pushing them around and to the side, like a kid trying to trick their parent into thinking they ate their veggies. A moment later, I glance up to find Luca emerging from the dark hallway, Jolie two steps behind him.

He straightens his tie—and stops in his tracks when he spots me.

My lips curl at the sides, and I lift a hand, giving a dainty finger wave. Surrounded by staff and customers, he paints a cordial smile on his face to compensate for the "oh shit" look in his eyes. Forever a man who loathes surprises. Running his hands down the lapels of his suit coat, he makes his way to my side of the room.

"Lydia," he says when he approaches my table. "Wasn't expecting to see you here."

"I've heard so many good things." I point to my mess of a salad. "Been wanting to try this place. Thought nothing could top the clam chowder your wife treated me to from your little deli yesterday, but this salad is to die for."

The space above his jaw divots. I must be such an inconvenience to this life he's built, a speed bump in his fast lane.

A male server walks by, doing a double take at the two of us, followed by a second, less nonchalant one. Perhaps Luca isn't the kind of restaurant owner who makes personal rounds and this is a new and exciting scene for the staff. Or maybe they're picking up on the stifling amount of tension that's suddenly filled the room?

"You having a good day so far?" I ask.

Seeing him so . . . *evolved* is nothing short of bizarre.

It's as if he's a completely different man—like the version he once was died along with me.

"Been busier than usual. Jolie said you wanted to talk to me?" He checks the diamond-encrusted timepiece on his wrist before returning his attention to me. I've yet to get a read on him, but with enough time, I'll get into that head of his.

"Yeah, actually." I pick at the tablecloth. "I've been thinking about my next move."

"I'd be happy to discuss that with you privately." His voice lowers. "Preferably in my home."

"I want a job." I cut to the chase. *"Here."*

He tries to speak, but I wag a finger.

"I'm thinking . . . assistant manager," I continue. "I want to help you run this place."

He scrunches his nose. "No. Absolutely not. That's a terrible idea."

Tilting my head, I adjust my linen napkin over my thighs. "Not sure if you know this, but it's pretty much impossible for a dead woman—or someone without any form of proper identification—to get a job. A legit job. With benefits and all that good stuff."

His focus whips from left to right before he leans over my table.

"You don't understand." His voice resides a hair above a whisper. "I'm in the process of cutting jobs. I can't be adding managerial positions we don't need."

"Sounds like we're both in a hard place," I say. "As soon as I sort out the death certificate business, I can get a real job. Until then, you're my only option."

"I'd love to help you, Lydia, but—"

"Look, you can close this place, walk out of here right now, and find work," I say. "If you don't do this for me, I'll be on the street. And could you really live with yourself if you let that happen, Luca? After everything I've been through? After the vows we took?"

He says nothing.

"Not to mention, people love to talk around here," I add. "It won't be long before people drag your name through the mud for abandoning your—"

His jaw flexes. "Fine."

I don't need to elaborate. He sees where I'm going with this.

"I can start Monday," I say. "And I'd like an office. A key. A computer. And a generous salary—under the table, of course. Because, well . . . you know."

His dark eyes narrow, as if he still doesn't quite know what to think of all this or what to do with me.

I lean close. "A thousand bucks a day to start should be sufficient."

It's an insane request. I know. But the way I look at it, I've lost out on almost a decade's worth of earnings, and with these menu prices, Luca's clearly in a position to help. Besides, it's not like I'm asking for his unborn son . . .

"I can't afford that." His voice is low as he glances over his shoulder.

"I've seen your menu." I shrug and push my limp salad around. "Pretty sure you can."

"I'm not paying you a thousand dollars a day."

"It'd be a couple of weeks. Three at most." I politely nod when I catch the curious eye of one of his servers. Surely he can spare twenty grand, even if it means putting that pretty little missus on a spending freeze.

He studies me with a gaze that could melt steel beams.

The Lydia he knew was never this audacious.

But time changes people. As does trauma. And captivity. And new-found freedom. For the entirety of my twenties, I wasn't allowed to ask for what I wanted, what I needed. All that changed the instant I was no longer under The Monster's rule.

I'm taking everything back now.

"You're putting me in an incredibly difficult position," he says, voice gruff and hardly above a whisper.

Behind him, Jolie carries a serving tray on her shoulder, headed our way with my overpriced surf and turf. I've already decided when the check arrives, I'll be sure to let Jolie know her boss is footing the bill today—along with a generous 30 percent tip.

"You're an astute businessman now, are you not?" I sip my water. "I'm sure you'll figure it out."

CHAPTER NINETEEN

I'm parked next to Luca's Maserati when I notice her. Dashing out the main entrance of Coletto's by the Sea, a little hop in her step and a hint of a smile on her face, is none other than Lydia—in the white coat and black boots from yesterday, no less.

There's no reason on God's green earth that she would be here—if she can't afford dollar-store tennis shoes, I can't imagine any scenario where she'd be dropping thirty bucks on a salad. And after Luca went off on me yesterday about being too generous, I doubt he invited her here for a comped meal.

Then again, he hasn't been himself lately.

I don't know that I'm qualified to know what he would *or* wouldn't do these days.

I bite my thumbnail, tasting salt, too preoccupied to be disgusted with myself.

Did Luca put that ridiculous smile on her face?

"Go see Daddy?" Elsie asks from her car seat, pointing to the white exterior of our beloved namesake restaurant. This is the one that started it all, that launched us to the moon and helped fund our other restaurant babies.

This place is special.

Sacred.

Raffi croons over the speakers. "Robin in the Rain." It's an unusually sunny February afternoon, and I thought we'd surprise Luca with a quick visit while we were out running errands. I figured seeing his wife and daughter might lift his spirits.

Guess I thought wrong . . .

"Not today, sweet pea." My voice breaks as I push the gear shifter into drive. "Daddy's busy. We'll see him tonight."

I exit the parking lot at the rear, managing to avoid Lydia as well as the window from Luca's office.

Heading home, I hold the wheel at a perfect ten and two, knuckles glossy white as my daughter sings and bops in the back seat, blissfully unaware of the raging inferno about to threaten this perfect life of ours.

Two miles down the road, I get held up at a train crossing. The black-and-yellow engine, with its aggressive blaring horn, pulls a never-ending line of graffiti-covered cargo. With nothing but time on my hands, I grab my phone from the charger and text my husband a simple note to ask how his day's going.

He reads it immediately.

He doesn't respond.

If it were any other day and I hadn't seen Lydia traipsing out of our restaurant, I'd assume he was held up at work. I wouldn't give it a second thought. I wouldn't torture myself with ominous worries about him trying to craft the perfect nonchalant response to cover whatever the hell he's doing behind my back.

Bile burns the back of my throat at the thought of Luca and Lydia having conversations without me—conversations that will affect *our* future.

The train clears the tracks, and the crossing arms lift. While Elsie sings along to a song about a peanut butter sandwich, the words "imbecile," "fool," and "naive" dance around in my head.

I'm just as much a part of this as he is.

We're a *team*.

What affects him affects me, too.

I pull into the garage ten minutes later, kill the engine, and sit paralyzed with thoughts until our unborn son kicks inside me. Luca should be home in four hours, which means I have two hundred and forty minutes to compose myself, to ensure that the moment he walks in the door tonight I won't say something I can never take back.

I'm hormonal, he's under an enormous amount of pressure at work, and the situation with Lydia is growing stranger by the moment.

This house of cards is one gust of wind from toppling over, and I don't want to be that gust.

CHAPTER TWENTY

LYDIA

"So I was thinking," Delphine says as I tend to the angel card rack with a feather duster. I'm not technically employed at The Blessed Alchemist, but her errands list for me today was slim, and I felt like being useful in any capacity was better than sitting around her apartment like some squatter. "How would next Wednesday work for the vital records office?"

I swallow, my back toward her as I remove the stack of Archangel Gabriel cards from their holder. This is the third time she's brought up the records office in the last twenty-four hours alone. She's not going to drop it.

"Actually, you know my friends the Colettos?" I keep my voice cordial. "They offered me a job at one of their restaurants, and I accepted it earlier today. They want me to start Monday. I'd hate to ask for time off the first week, you know? Once I get settled, we can figure out the perfect time to take care of that."

"Angel, that's *wonderful*." I turn and find Delphine dancing on her toes, clapping her hands together, like my luck is her luck.

That or she's relieved that she no longer has to offer me a job—perhaps she was having second thoughts.

"You know, you're still welcome to work for me, too," she says, tamping down her excitement and putting on her businesswoman hat.

"He's willing to pay me under the table until everything gets sorted out," I say. "As a personal favor. I don't want to put you in that position . . ."

"Of course, of course." She tugs at the moldavite piece hanging from her slender neck. "Just wanted you to know my offer still stands if it doesn't work out for some reason."

Lately she's been going above and beyond for me. Just last night, she asked me my favorite meal—chicken potpie—and then cooked it from scratch. I'd have been happy with the ninety-nine-cent microwave version, but she ran to the store and came back with bags of ingredients and spent an hour assembling everything while telling me about the time Amber made jambalaya simply because she loved the word and almost burned the kitchen down.

Just this morning, she invited me to join her for sunrise yoga and patiently taught me eight beginner positions. I can't think of a single instance in my childhood when my mom taught me anything. In the short time I've known this woman, she's done more for me than my own mother did in the eighteen years we shared together. I have nothing to give Delphine in return except for my companionship.

And I'd hardly call that even stephen.

I finish the angel card rack when my phone buzzes in my back pocket—a sensation that sends a shock to my chest because I'm still not quite used to it. Flipping it open, I'm greeted with a text from Merritt, asking if I'm free to get together this afternoon.

I text back, asking her to name the time and the place.

A few minutes later, she writes back, Pick you up at 3!

"I was thinking maybe coffee and dessert at one of our restaurants?" Merritt says when I climb inside her car that afternoon. "We've got the best cinnamon chocolate soufflé at sea bats."

"Sea bats?" I ask, not understanding.

"Sorry." She chuckles, sweeping a glossy wave off her shoulder. "That's what we call our flagship—Coletto's by the Sea. C.B.T.S. Anyway, you're going to love it, I promise."

Shit.

She coasts us through a green light, tapping her fingers against the steering wheel to some Hall and Oates song, and all I can think about is what if the hostess recognizes me from earlier today? What if we get the same server? Safe to say Luca hasn't told her about the job yet, or she wouldn't be so giddy about introducing me to their flagship restaurant. This has the potential to get awkward.

I'm baking alive in this puffy white coat, so I undo the zipper and gather a lungful of new car scent.

"Isn't that your nicest one?" I ask. "I'd be fine with just going to a regular coffee shop . . ."

She swats a hand. "Don't be ridiculous. People drive hours for our soufflé alone. I'm telling you, you won't be sorry."

"I don't know if I'm dressed for . . . *sea bats.*"

She chuffs. "What are they going to do, turn you away? Luca would never allow that. And neither would I. You're our guest."

I may be many things, but reducing my presence in their life to guest status is a slap in the face.

A minute later, we're parking outside the familiar white-shingled building with the impeccable ocean views. I don't feel the ground beneath my feet as we walk inside, and I shove my sweaty palms into my fluffy pockets, keeping my chin tucked like it could make me less noticeable.

"Astrid, hi," she greets the hostess—the same girl who seated me a few hours earlier. "So wonderful to see you today. Could we get table nine, please? And we're just doing coffee and dessert today, so we won't need the full menu."

I avoid making eye contact with the young woman, whose gaze darts between our faces as she slowly reaches for two small menus, silver printed on black.

"O-of course, Mrs. Coletto," she says with a stammer. "Right this way."

I hold my breath the entire walk to table number nine, and I release it when she leaves us be without blowing my cover.

"It's beautiful in here," I say, ignoring the menu and peering around the expansive place like it's my first time. "Love the light fixtures."

"Vintage Spectra crystal," she says with a rich gleam in her eye. "We pulled them from an old restaurant back in Maryland, one of my mom's favorites. They were tearing it down, and I couldn't let them go to waste. All they needed was a good polishing. Plus it's nice to have a part of her here, watching over us in a way, as strange as that sounds."

Our eyes hold across the table.

"Good afternoon, ladies," a male server says as he approaches our table. "Mrs. Coletto, haven't seen you in a while."

"Levi." She reaches, brushing her hand against his arm. "How's the boyfriend?"

"Amazing." He beams from one ear to the next. "Going on six months now."

"Told you." She winks.

"What are we having today?" he asks with the besotted smile of a payroll kiss-ass.

"Coffee and two chocolate soufflés," she says. "Oh. Decaf for me."

"Of course." His attention flips to me as he takes my menu, and his deep-set gaze widens. He was one of the gawkers earlier, one of the servers who slow-walked past Luca and me in the midst of our exchange. Tucking the menus under his arm, he says, "I'll be right back with those."

If it weren't so dim in here thanks to the fading afternoon sun, I'm positive she'd be able to see all the sweat that's collected above my brow in the past five minutes. Should Merritt find out I was here once already today and didn't breathe a word about it as we pulled into the parking lot, there's nothing I can possibly say to excuse that. It's not like there are multiple *sea bats* in Bent Creek or that I've got a shoddy short-term memory to blame it on.

Levi returns with two carafes of coffee—one in polished silver, the other a matte gold. He places the silver one in front of Merritt, along with a pristine white teacup on a floral saucer.

"Decaf for the mother-to-be," he says with a sweet smile that fades when he meets my gaze. "And this one's regular. Give us about thirty minutes for those soufflés, ladies."

He doesn't turn *my* teacup right side up.

I pour my own coffee, and when it's cool enough to take a sip, I close my eyes and smile. "This coffee is . . . something else."

Truth is, I've had day-old gas station coffee that tasted better than this.

She bats a hand. "Little trade secret for you, but this is the same coffee we serve at The Coastal Commissary. Same brand and machines and everything. I'm convinced the fancy cup makes it taste better. Packaging is everything."

"Interesting." And it is. If I didn't know better, I'd suspect she's bragging about ripping off the very same customers who pay her bills.

"It's a shame," she says. "We have to shutter those doors. Coffee shops aren't as profitable as one might think. A lot of overhead involved, at least in the early years. Looking back now, our location wasn't ideal—we were inside a theater. Most of the tourists in town, they go to the Starbucks and The Coffee Bean & Tea Leaf—familiar places. And the locals, they tend to gravitate toward the big corner shops with the impossible-to-miss signs and the outdoor seating."

"It must be hard," I say, "running all those businesses."

My attention is laser focused, ready to digest any tidbit of information she throws my way, fully prepared to read between each and every line as if my life depends on it—because in a way, it does. Are they truly struggling? Or are they funneling their money and energy into their most profitable business models? I read once that financial struggles were one of the leading causes of divorce, second only to sexual dissatisfaction.

Judging by the bulbous bump protruding from her Pilates body, I'd say their bedroom life is a nonissue.

"A lot of it is learning as you go." She sips her decaf, leaving a mark of nude-pink lipstick on the edge. "Everyone makes mistakes, though. It's just how it is."

"Do you have help?"

Merritt shakes her head. "Luca prefers to do it all himself. He's a bit of a control freak when it comes to the restaurants. Heck, it took him months to find a new manager for the deli last year. He always has to find that one perfect person he can mold into exactly what he wants."

"This place must be doing amazing, though." I nod toward the floor-to-ceiling windows that showcase a glimmering Pacific seascape. "It's stunning. Certainly the most beautiful restaurant *I've* set foot in."

Which isn't saying much . . .

This location with its epic view. The parking lot full of luxury imports. The soul-sucking prices on the menu. It's a restaurateur's wet dream.

She takes another sip, hesitating, examining me for a second. "We do all right."

We.

"Hey, you." Luca's familiar velvet tenor cuts through our conversation without warning.

"Hey." Her pink lips curl up at the sides, and a twinkle colors her pale irises.

"You didn't tell me you were stopping by." He stoops as if he's going to kiss the top of her head only to change course at the final second.

"Last-minute decision." She shrugs.

"Where's Elsie?" he asks. While he speaks to her, he gifts me with a squinted gaze. Is he curious? Captivated? Concerned? I can't read him like I used to, but his attention is where it should be, and that's all that matters.

"With Annette, who else?" Merritt releases a nervous chuckle, waving her hand as if it's some magic wand that could wave off this obvious tension brewing between Luca and me. "Such silly questions today."

"My apologies. I thought Annette had the day off." His voice is canned, robotic almost.

They exchange looks before redirecting their attention to me in tandem. All this feels like bad acting, theatrical. And it's understandable with all this uncertainty looming over their beautiful life.

"Did Luca tell you he hired me?" I ask since we're all together anyway—and if their marriage is the stuff that fairy tales are made of, there shouldn't be any secrets.

Merritt sits her teacup on its saucer with a loud clink, nearly missing the center. "I'm sorry?"

"I start Monday." I volunteer the next bit, as the cat seems to have Luca's tongue as per usual. "Assistant manager."

Her lips waver. "Is that true, Luca? I thought . . . I . . . I'm just . . . I'm . . . this is news to me."

"Still waiting to get the official go-ahead from our accountant." He lies to his wife in a way that feels oddly natural, as if he's accustomed to placating her. And then he places his hand on her shoulder, though his attention is very much directed to me. I know this look. He isn't pleased. "Was going to tell you tonight."

"Mr. Coletto, I'm so sorry to interrupt, but you have a phone call on line two," a petite auburn-haired server says with a wince. "It's the lobster vendor."

"Ah, yes. I've been waiting for that call. Ladies, enjoy your coffee." He steals one final glimpse in my direction, letting it linger for a second too long. "Mer, I'll see you at home."

Without a response, her lips press flat, and she buries her expression with a sip of decaf coffee.

She isn't pleased.

"I'm so sorry," I say. "I shouldn't have blurted it like that . . . he told me it wasn't official, but I was so excited . . . I guess I just assumed the two of you had already talked about it . . ."

Her fingers tremble around her cup.

"Are you okay?" I ask.

And I *am* sorry . . . I'm sorry she's in the middle of this. It isn't her fault she got the older, wiser, more successful version of the man I married. Some people are simply born lucky. I'd even go so far as to place her in the same category as Delphine with her generosity and sweet, trusting nature. She doesn't deserve the strife. Fortunately my presence in her life is only temporary.

"I'm so sorry if I upset you," I say.

"No need to apologize," Merritt says, propping herself up and painting a subtle smile on her face. "Just caught off guard, is all. I'm sure he would've told me tonight."

I take a drink. "Yes, of course. I'm sure he would've."

Levi delivers our chocolate soufflés, which are admittedly amazing. Maybe the only item worth a damn on this whole menu.

We finish our afternoon treat with small talk, safe generic topics only. Topics so boring they could make the wallpaper peel.

"Have to say, I'm enjoying getting to know you, Lydia. More than I expected I would, given the circumstances," she says, shepherding me to the exit when it's over. I told her I wanted to walk home, to burn off these sugary calories and enjoy this rare sunny day we're having. And I swear I spotted a hint of relief on her pretty face, as if she'd been waiting for the moment she could rid herself of my company and have a word with her husband.

Our husband.

"Same," I say. "We should do this again soon." I eye her belly. "Before you pop."

She laughs, smoothing a hand along her bump. "Yes. Soon."

I show myself out, but before I make it across the threshold, I catch her making a beeline for his office.

I'd kill to be a fly on that wall.

CHAPTER
TWENTY-ONE

MERRITT

"Hey," Luca says when I appear in his office doorway. He doesn't glance away from his computer. Instead, he clacks at his keyboard and clicks his mouse, frowning at the monitor. "Shut the door, will you?"

It takes all the restraint I have not to slam it.

"You *hired* her?" I collapse into the guest chair across from his desk. "You told me we weren't in a position to help her, and then you go and do this . . . *behind my back*? After berating me last night for a similar suggestion?"

"I thought about what you said, about helping her get on her feet so she'd move on." He toys with a pen, his stare fixed on a framed family portrait on the corner of his desk. "And I think you're right."

I know I'm right. I'm *always* right.

Which also adds another level of concern to this entire situation, seeing as how my husband can't keep his eyes off Lydia any time he's in her presence. It's as if he's transfixed, besotted.

"So now we magically have money again?" I focus on the issue at hand.

His mouth forms a straight line. "No."

"My God, Luca." I rest my elbow on the ledge of the chair and bury my face in my hands. "We're laying off staff. We're in a hiring freeze. We're—"

"I *know*."

Earlier he insisted he was going to tell me tonight.

Now I'll never know if that's true.

When I spotted her dashing out of the restaurant earlier, my original plan was to wait it out, to see if he'd mention her little visit after he got home from work. But thinking about it got me too worked up, to the point that I couldn't calm down. Racing and sweating and pacing all over the house. The way I saw it, I had two options: either suffer through it all day until my husband got home . . . or get ahead of the storm. Impatience got the best of me, and within minutes, I was texting Lydia about meeting up and calling Annette to have her watch Elsie for a couple of hours.

But out of all the bombshells, I wasn't expecting *that* one. Never in a million years did I think he'd make a decision like that without at least running it by me first. It's not like he's buying her shoes—he's giving her a job. At our *only* profitable restaurant. Which happens to house his main office, where he spends forty-plus hours a week.

He's edging me out of this equation—why?

My middle tightens, a mild Braxton-Hicks contraction. Or maybe indigestion. It's hard to tell this late in the game. I breathe through it, eyes shut tight, waiting for it to pass. Luca rises from his leather chair so quickly it hits the back wall, and he drops to my side.

"You okay?" he asks.

I miss this side of him—the attentive, doting husband.

The contraction subsides, but I breathe a little harder and shut my eyes a little tighter. I need his sympathy. I deserve his concern. It's the least he can do after this shit show of a day.

Taking my hand, he lifts it to his lips and deposits a distraction in the form of a kiss.

"Go. Rest," he says. "Put your feet up. I'll be home soon."

He helps me out of the guest chair and escorts me all the way to my car. Either he's being a gentleman to make up for his actions . . . or he wants to guarantee I leave the premises.

I drive home, half-blinded by tears that fall far too easily these days.

Hormonal or not, I know one thing: I'm losing him.

Piece by piece, day by day, lie by lie.

Everything I do is for Luca, for our marriage, for our children, for our life, for our future. Anything I've ever kept from him has been for his own good.

Now I can't help but wonder if he could say the same.

CHAPTER TWENTY-TWO

LYDIA

"I'm going to need an identity of some kind," I tell Luca Monday afternoon, when he slides a fat envelope across my assistant manager's desk. It's a tiny office, the size of a bathroom maybe. A desk, a computer, no windows. It reeks of stale kitchen scents and could use a more comfortable chair, but I demanded, he delivered, and that's all that matters.

"What are you talking about?" He shuts the door.

"I'd love to, you know, open a bank account to put this money in at some point." In any other scenario, it would be wrong to accept a thousand bucks in cash for literally sitting on my ass all day browsing the internet. But given the last nine years and everything I've missed out on, my conscience is happily making an exception. "Kind of need that so I can get an apartment . . . a car . . . basic life things."

His hands rest at his narrow hips. "How've you been getting by the last several months?"

"Oh, you mean grifting and working under-the-table jobs for pennies on the dollar? Hired by people who had no qualms about taking advantage of my situation?" I don't blink, don't miss a beat. "Sleeping in homeless shelters and on park benches?" I lean forward, elbows sliding across my desk. "I'm done surviving, Luca. I want to *live*."

His shoulders slump, and he drags a hand through his hair, which catches on his polished wedding band.

I don't envy this man.

Merritt is his rock, and I'm his hard place—he's caught between us.

"Listen, I know this arrangement isn't going to last forever," I say. "Nor do I want to have to come in here and see your face five days a week, because it represents some life truths I don't want to have to think about on a regular basis. *But* . . . this is the way it has to be. I've thought about this from every angle, and this is the simplest way to make this fair."

His lack of response is a silent agreement.

He doesn't need to know I've no plans to use the stolen identity I'm requesting—I simply need to buy time so I can continue to save money, and this was a logical solution given my extraordinarily unusual circumstances. It's not like he can strut down to the big box store on the south side of town in his Italian leather loafers, slap down his black AmEx, and order me a new identity. The longer this takes, the more thousand-dollar paydays I'll collect, and the closer I'll be to living out the rest of my life the way it was always supposed to be.

No one ever said life was fair, and I'm living proof.

"If you don't mind, I should probably get back to work," I say with a wink. Pointing to the door and making a shooing motion with my hand, I add, "Close it on your way, please."

Luca lingers, studying me with a quiet intensity as if he's taking me in for the first time all over again.

And then he's gone.

I can't imagine the cocktail of thoughts filling his head. If he'd have an actual conversation with me, I'd be happy to tell him there's no sense in worrying. Everything's going to work out exactly the way it should.

For everyone.

CHAPTER
TWENTY-THREE

MERRITT

"All I ever wanted was a family of my own," I tell Lydia over lunch Tuesday afternoon. I haven't seen her since last week, but I've driven past the restaurant every day, hoping to catch a glimpse of something—though I don't know what.

Today I stopped in to say hello to my husband and happened to catch his first wife on break in her office—alone, thank God. On a whim, I had the chef whip up a couple of lobster mac and cheeses and cozied up to her desk for an impromptu lunch date.

The baby is scheduled to arrive next Wednesday, the C-section planned for eight AM with a check-in at seven. I have a week to get to know Lydia better, to vet out what she *really* wants, and to show her I'm only human in hopes that she won't do anything to tear my beautiful little family apart.

"My mother was something else," I say. "I was always so in awe of her. She had this larger-than-life presence about her. And not just because she was gorgeous. I mean, she was, but that wasn't where her strength lay. She was the kind of person who refused to take crap from anyone. She had this invisible steely exterior. You couldn't offend her, couldn't hurt her. It also made her a little distant, you know? Hard to get to know. I admired her as a woman, but I always thought I could do a little better as a mother."

"And are you?" Lydia asks. "Are you a better mother than she was?"

"I like to think so, yes." I dab my lips, leaving a tinge of scarlet lipstick on the napkin. "She once told me that she loved us in an obligatory way, that she was doing the best she could. Having children was fulfilling a marital expectation. Her generation was like that, I think. It's just what you did back then. Anyway, she sent us away to boarding school the first chance she got. And I spent a lot of years hating her for it—wishing she could be a quote-unquote normal mother. Only now, I realize there's no such thing. Only people trying their best at an impossible job."

I pause to take a bite, hoping my words sink in. Opening up to people isn't a forte of mine, but if this means securing the safety of my family, I'll do it.

My mother took her own life the day after my eighteenth birthday—sleeping pills and a steady stream of carbon monoxide courtesy of her champagne-gold Aston Martin. I realized then that it didn't matter how strong a person was, how resistant they were to criticism and judgment—life could still wear a person down if they weren't in their own driver's seat. At least she died in hers.

My mother had a beautiful life—but it was never one that she had an ounce of control over.

My father had full command over that ship, which is why I've purposely built our marital relationship on equal grounds. There's a fine line between loving someone and submitting to them. It requires balance, intention, and action. I like to think I've mastered it thus far. God forbid my efforts go to waste.

"What about your mother—is she still around?" I ask, not wanting to dominate the conversation too obviously.

"She died when I was in high school." There's no emotion in Lydia's voice, not even a hint of a wince on her plain face.

"I'm so sorry." I stretch a hand over her desk but she withdraws, reaching for her water. "It's nice to have things in common with someone, but not *these* types of things."

"She was weak," Lydia says with zero emotion in her voice. "It was bound to happen sooner or later."

I don't ask the details—it isn't polite to pry. Besides, her lunch break is ending soon, and I need to wrap this up and leave on a powerful note.

"Luca had a terrible childhood; you know that, right?" I focus on my husband next, building sympathy for him as well. "His parents were just awful to him. He hasn't spoken to them in years. I've only met them once. He won't let them anywhere near Elsie. He's so protective of her."

"Yes, he'd told me all about them when we were married," Lydia says. Her stare floats to the side, as if she's reminiscing.

"Can you imagine how awful it must've been for him?" I ask. "To be the only child of a narcissist and an alcoholic?"

She nods, exhaling. "Thank goodness he isn't anything like them."

"I know, right? He's worked so hard to overcome some of his issues. To break the cycle."

"I see that." Her thin lips work into a sliver of a smile. "Though I imagine neither of us knows the half of what he went through."

"Can we ever truly know everything about everyone?"

"No," she says. "I don't think we can."

CHAPTER
TWENTY-FOUR

L Y D I A

"Oh, my goodness, angel. You don't have to keep doing this for me." Delphine palms her cheeks when I arrive home Wednesday night with a takeout bag—third night in a row. Every afternoon, I tell the chef to prepare a to-go entrée for me. Only it's never for me. After everything this woman has done for me, a few fancy meals courtesy of *sea bats* is the least I can give her in return. "I've never eaten so well in my life."

She slicks her hands together, and I set the table. The food is more than enough for the both of us and then some. My stomach can only handle so much richness, and Delphine isn't the type to overindulge. I won't do this indefinitely, but it's a little something-something for now.

"So how's it going so far?" she asks as we dig into our respective piles of fettucine alfredo with Pacific geoduck clams—whatever those are. "Staff keeping you on your toes?"

"It's mostly office work—ordering supplies, taking inventory, double-checking scheduling," I lie. And it pains me to lie. But I can't tell her the truth, that I sit in the office with the door closed all day, browsing the internet or doing printed-off crossword puzzles to pass the time.

Luca refuses to give me actual work to do, though I can't figure out why. Any time I ask if I can be of service, he mutters something about taking a phone call or letting me know and disappears. He's clearly avoiding me, trying to busy himself enough to forget I'm back.

Unfortunately for him, I'm not going anywhere.

Not for a while.

"Boring stuff." I twirl a small mountain of pasta on my fork. "I was going to ask you . . . how much should I pay you for rent now?"

She rests her fork against her plate and sits back, as if the thought had yet to cross her mind. But I'm not going to live here scot-free and take advantage of her.

"I can still do laundry and those kinds of things if you want," I add. "Would just have to be after hours."

Lord knows I've got nothing but time.

"You haven't even had your first paycheck yet, angel." Her voice is as tender as the veal they serve at *sea bats* on Tuesdays. "One thing at a time. Let me think on that and get back to you with a number."

My mind wanders to the three thousand in cash tucked into the interior pocket of my backpack. It isn't safe to haul that kind of money around. Tonight I'll stick most of it in the dresser, under a stack of folded sweaters. Come Friday, that money will be almost doubled, and by next week, I'll have an entire drawer full of it—which isn't practical.

Yesterday I suffered through a depressing lunch with Merritt. She was gaming for compassion, sharing sob stories about her dead mother. But there aren't enough dead moms in the world to make me walk away now, when I'm so close to the flipside of hell.

I didn't spend nine years in captivity to spend the next fifty of them homeless.

Even if I liked Merritt, even if I *adored* her—it couldn't stop me from doing what I came here to do . . . what I *have* to do.

CHAPTER
TWENTY-FIVE

"Seven days." I fold the baby's coming-home outfit and place it inside the hospital bag. "Can you believe it?"

Luca hasn't said more than two words since he got home from work, and the circles under his eyes are getting darker by the minute. But I waited to pack the bags until now, hoping it'd give him a little something to look forward to. A roundabout reminder that life is still moving forward all around us. Good things are on the horizon.

I tug the zipper and place the duffel by our bedroom door, that way he'll see it every time he comes and goes. The more reminders of what's at stake, the better.

I want my husband back—my true husband. The man I married, not his speechless, secretive doppelgänger.

"Luca?" I shuffle back to the bed.

"Hmm?" He glances up from his phone, eyes squinted and swollen with exhaustion. He hasn't been sleeping, and I know this because neither have I.

I climb in beside him, wedge beneath the covers, and gently remove the phone from his hand.

"I miss you," I whisper. It's a strange thing to say to someone who's right beside me, but I don't know how else to convey to him that lately he's here . . . but he isn't. "Are you okay? Because I don't think you are."

He won't make eye contact, he simply stares out the window on the far wall, into a literal ocean of blackness.

"This isn't easy for me." His tone is so unconvincing it's insulting. It's as if he's simply uttering the words but his mind is elsewhere . . . with someone else.

With her.

"I'm doing my best," he adds.

"*This* is your best?" I breathe. My patience is wearing paper thin. I can't stand another minute living in this gray area, not knowing what Lydia wants or what my husband is thinking—or doing—half of the time. "Zoned out? Detached?"

He rustles, changing his posture and clearing his throat. Without a word, he slips his arm around my shoulders and pulls me in. A moment later, his warm lips press against my forehead—never my lips anymore. It's as if the man I love is slipping through my fingers.

I lean away. "Yeah, well. I'm afraid *this* isn't going to work this time."

His forehead creases. "I don't understand."

"You can't just . . . hold my hand or kiss me every time I'm upset and expect it to fix everything. We need to have a conversation—the one you've been sidestepping." I turn away long enough to blink away the threat of tears.

He blows a hard, cinnamon-toothpaste-scented breath, massaging the tension from his face as his shoulders sag. "I've been preoccupied, Mer. Yes. But there's nothing to fix here. Nothing is broken. I'm not going anywhere; you're not going anywhere. We're having this baby, and everything else we'll take one day at a time."

"Everything else meaning . . . Lydia." It's not a question.

"Lydia . . . the business . . . everything that isn't you and Elsie and the baby." He reaches for my hand, threading his fingers in mine. His skin is ice cold. "Trust me. Everything's going to go back to the way it was before."

It's the only thing I want—and the only thing I've ever wanted.

I switch off the lamp on the nightstand and return to my husband's side, resting a little easier tonight knowing we're on the same page.

CHAPTER TWENTY-SIX

LYDIA

Luca's Maserati is mysteriously absent from the parking lot Thursday morning, and when I head in, I find his office door locked, no light peeking out from under the door. Heading to the galley to find someone who knows where he is, I stop outside the doorway when I overhear a hushed conversation.

"Did you hear he closed the coffee shop?" one of them asks. "No warning or anything. Just walked in last week, emptied the register, and told everyone to go home."

"You're kidding," the other one gasps. "I knew they were shutting down Salt and Sky, and I heard the deli wasn't doing so hot, but I didn't know The Commissary was on the chopping block."

"Wonder if we're next . . ."

"He just hired an assistant manager," the first one says. "Pretty sure that means we're doing okay."

"Yeah, speaking of her. Where the hell did she come from? And why wouldn't he just pull the manager from The Commissary or whatever? Pretty messed up."

"I don't even know what she does here," a third one interjects. "She's in her office all day. Only comes out to get something to drink or talk to Luca for a second, then she disappears. Something's not adding up . . ."

"Maybe she's going to save the restaurants?" the first one asks. "Maybe she's some kind of financial consultant, and she's moving numbers."

I stifle a chuckle. This amuses me more than it should.

"Consultants aren't cheap, though," he continues.

"Yeah, but neither is that mansion of his . . ." the second one says under a cough.

The three of them laugh, and I use the opportunity to step out of the hallway and into the light. "Sorry to interrupt, but have any of you heard from Mr. Coletto today?"

Their smiles fade in unison. Two of them look away.

"His wife had their baby last night," the first one tells me. "He's not coming in today."

Holy shit.

I didn't think she was due until next week.

My stomach drops to my feet, and my breath hitches. Despite knowing this was going to happen sooner than later, the reality of the news leaves a bittersweet taste on my tongue.

"Lovely." I infuse my tone with pleasantness, feigning happiness for my husband and his missus. "Guess I'm in charge today. If any of you need anything, you know where to find me."

By ten o'clock, I'm browsing apartments online. I want to give Delphine some kind of compensation for room and board, but I've no idea what a decent place in this area goes for. Judging by a handful of comps, I deduce that she's paying somewhere around a thousand bucks a month for her place above the shop.

With Luca out today, I likely won't be getting today's cut. But when I get home, I'll set aside five hundred for her.

Out of curiosity, I click around on a few other listings, scrolling through sunlit, staged pictures and imagining one day having a place of my own. Not in Bent Creek, of course. This town is ruined for me. But somewhere perpetually warm, with more sunshine and less rain. Palm trees instead of evergreens. The desert, perhaps.

It's two o'clock when I decide to throw in the towel. I don't know how people can sit in front of computers all day, every day and not want to gouge their eyes out. Every blink feels like sandpaper against my eyelids, and when I push myself up from my chair, my bones creak and pop.

Grabbing my backpack, I lock up the office and head out—catching a handful of nosy stares from staff. I pass their coffee shop on the way—pausing to read the PERMANENTLY CLOSED sign posted in the window. My heart goes out to the staff, the innocent bystanders of Luca's entrepreneurial greed. I can only hope my thousand-bucks-a-day "salary" didn't accelerate that closing.

Taking a detour, I head for the boutique district, wasting the remainder of the afternoon wandering through bookshops and candle stores and coming out of it all with a few new clothes from a place called The Modern Lily. Spending money is something I look forward to getting used to again. Might as well start today.

It's shortly after six by the time I get to the apartment. Delphine's already closed the shop for the evening. Trekking the back stairs with shopping bags and zero food in hand, I prep myself with an apology in case she was expecting another *sea bats* meal . . .

Bracing myself to deliver disappointment on an invisible platter, I head inside—only to be met with Delphine seated at the kitchen table, hands folded next to stacks upon stacks of cash.

"Lydia." There's no sugar-spun softness in her voice this time.

Powder scampers across the kitchen, weaving between my legs before darting off, hiding.

Her gaze drifts to the money, then to me.

I take the seat across from her, my heart sinking. I can only imagine what's going through her mind. No one has this kind of cash shoved in a drawer—no one but drug dealers and career criminals.

I don't ask why she was rifling through my drawers. They were never mine to begin with. None of this was. I was only ever a guest under her roof, eating off her vintage silverware, drinking her non-GMO coffee, and wearing her dead daughter's clothes.

Drawing in a hard breath, I rest my elbows on the table, rake my fingers through my food-service-scented hair, and meet her scrutinizing stare. There's no way to know if I'll still be in her good graces by the end of this—or if I'll be right back where I started: homeless, penniless, and as good as dead.

Either way, she deserves to know everything.

"Care to explain what you're doing with all this cash?" She blinks.

I've told the story to myself a million times, practicing it like a script on sleepless nights. Playing it out like a movie in my head. Wondering where I begin. Does it start the moment I met my husband? Does it begin on that perfectly beautiful summer day, the moment my freedom was snatched without warning?

I don't suppose it matters anymore.

I drag in another breath that rattles in my chest, squeeze my eyes tight, and lick the numbness from my lips.

"Ten years ago, I met a man." My throat thickens, and I interlace my fingers until my knuckles whiten. "We worked together at a diner, back in my hometown—Greenbrook, Washington. We dated for a few months. Inseparable. We were that stereotypical young, dumb, and crazy-in-love couple. Ended up eloping in Vegas one weekend. After that, he convinced me to move with him to Bent Creek—this sleepy little tourist town where his grandfather used to live. He had nothing but fond memories, told me we could find a nice restaurant and make a killing in tips. So we came here with nothing but the clothes on our backs. Found a fully furnished apartment on the east side of town for five hundred bucks a month. Eventually we were going to enroll in the community college, you know, once we were settled."

Delphine's slender fingertips lift to her mouth as she listens.

"And we were getting there," I continue. "We'd been here not quite three months, and everything was going exactly the way we planned . . . before I was taken."

She sits straight, hands falling to her lap in near slow motion. "Taken?"

I point to her phone on the counter. "You can google me. If you search *Lydia Coletto Bent Creek missing woman*, I'm the top result."

She eyes her device but doesn't move.

"I went out for a hike one Sunday afternoon," I say. "Alone. Like I always did. Left my husband a note on the kitchen table telling him I'd be back. But an hour into my hike, someone snuck up behind me. Grabbed me. Pinned me. Knocked me out with what I can only assume was chloroform or something similar. When I woke up, I was in a small, dark cabin. Zip ties on my wrists and ankles."

Delphine massages her lips together, her gaze pinched in my direction.

"For nine years, he held me captive in that little shack in the woods," I continue. "I'd be left for several days at a time usually. He'd come back to empty my waste bucket and give me just enough food and water to keep me alive so he could torture me—physically, sexually, psychologically." I wring my hands and inhale a cavernous breath so deep it burns. "I've blocked a lot of it out . . . learned early on how to leave my body."

I rise and lift the left hem of my shirt just above my midriff, showing her a handful of fading scars and various marks, a half dozen souvenirs of The Monster's abuse. Turning, I pull the right side higher, until she can read the name my captor carved into me with an X-Acto knife, which was surprisingly less painful than the hot lighters he'd pressed against my inner thighs the week before.

Delphine leans forward, squinting as she reads. "L-U-C-A."

I cover my bare skin and take a seat again, rapping my fingertips against the tabletop in quick succession, momentarily trapped in a memory.

"He carved his name into me," I say. "Branded me. Like a piece of property. He said I needed something to remember him by when he wasn't there reminding me . . ."

She lifts a palm. "Wait a minute. *Luca.* Is that the same Luca you visited the other day? The *friend* who offered you a job?"

I study her face, a feeble attempt to gauge her reaction. I wouldn't blame her if she didn't believe me. There are times I, too, wonder if it was all a dream—a nightmare.

"Yes," I say. "Turns out the man I married . . . was nothing more than a monster."

"Wait—Luca was your *husband*?" Her eyes glow wild with natural disbelief that I don't take personally.

"He was." I peer into my lap, folding my hands before picking at a hangnail until it bleeds. "I loved him. Or at least I thought I did." An endless bout of silence circles between us. "I've tried to make sense of it a million times. The only thing I can think of is that he was playing out some sick sexual fantasy of his. That the man I met and fell in love with was nothing more than an act. He lured me to Bent Creek with false promises of a beautiful life together, and then he waited for the right opportunity to do what he'd always planned to do. He let it slip one day that the cabin belonged to his grandfather, that he inherited it after his death years before. Everything he did had been planned. He was just waiting for the right girl to come along so he could execute it."

She nods, quiet for another beat as she digests this. "How did he know where you were that day?"

With a hand pressed against my lips, I exhale. "There was a GPS tracking device on my backpack. A lot of hikers have them. It's a safety thing. He would've known exactly where I was."

"Sick bastard."

"Among other things . . ."

Rising from the table, I fetch a glass of water to tamp down the nausea in my middle.

"For the first few weeks, he'd show up with that day's paper," I say. "I'll never forget that first headline . . . MISSING BENT CREEK NEWLYWED . . . and below that was a blown-up picture from our Vegas wedding. He then proceeded to read the article out loud, grinning wider than a Cheshire cat during the parts that painted him as a grief-stricken husband worried sick about his missing bride. The entire thing was bullshit. Every word of it." I return to the table. "I mean, it was but it wasn't. The lies he fed them were the same ones he fed to me. Telling them all about the life we had planned. How I was going to nursing school in the fall. And we were going to open a restaurant someday. That we had big plans for our future. And how we were wild about each other. Even called us soul mates."

There are days when the entire thing is shrouded in a dreamlike haze, days when I find myself wondering if any part of those first few months was real. They say first loves are intense, that they can hook their horns in parts of your heart you never knew existed and make you blind to reality. I'd be lying if I said I didn't fantasize about our exquisite early years, missing them with confusing intensity.

The Luca I knew from our diner days was quiet and docile. Always kept to himself. Stealing looks and gifting the occasional smile in passing until he finally worked up the nerve to approach me during a break one slow Thursday afternoon. With little finesse and a load of awkwardness, he asked if I wanted to catch a movie with him that weekend.

At first I told him no. Politely, of course. But the crestfallen look on his face haunted me for days, snapping my heart in two every time I thought about it.

I convinced myself I did the right thing.

He wasn't my type—not that I dated much. I was freshly twenty and had better things to do than find some local boy to chain myself to. But I tended to go for the louder guys, the ones who weren't afraid to make their presence known, who weren't satisfied with blending into the wallpaper. The ones who cracked witty one-liners, worked on cars, and repeated movie lines with impressive accuracy.

There was a darkness about Luca, an intensity I couldn't ignore. Some days I felt sorry for the guy, knowing full well what it's like to be an outsider myself. Other times I couldn't shake the frigid blast that blanketed the room in his presence. Even his stare would make me lose my train of thought sometimes.

I shamed myself for being dramatic, for viewing him the same way everyone else did.

I convinced myself he was simply misunderstood.

A misfit like me.

As time went on, any time the kitchen staff poked fun at him behind his back, I didn't hesitate to defend him. Everything about him screamed bully material, and I've always had a soft spot for the underdog.

It wasn't until a month later—on a rainy night when I hitched a ride home with him and we ended up driving around town for two hours—that we really got to talk. It was almost like being with an old friend.

Turned out all he needed was to be on his own turf. Seated comfortably behind the wheel of his car, he waxed on about fascinating conspiracy theories, classic literary fiction, cryptocurrency, AI, and the dark web. All this time I had thought he was void of personality, but all it took was a little change of scenery and the real Luca had a chance to shine.

I like your brain, I told him when he dropped me off later that night. *It's different.*

We sat in his idling car and he laughed, telling me it was a weird thing to say to someone but he'd accept the compliment anyway. I let him take me to that movie the following weekend. We were inseparable after that.

"He had me legally declared dead," I say, breaking our silence. "A couple years after I went *missing*."

Delphine chuffs. "Why would he do that?"

"Impossible to know." I lift a shoulder. "I only have theories."

Every twisted move Luca made was an exercise in power and control. I eventually learned—after endless hours of letting him yammer on about himself—that his parents were hyperzealous control freaks who held him to impossible OCD standards and rigid, militaristic schedules. The other day Merritt described them as alcoholic and narcissistic. And maybe that's the way he portrayed them to her. Either way, there's no denying Luca's the progeny of two unstable people, and *I* was the vessel for his rebellion—as were his messy mane, unkemptness, and penchant for torturing the helpless.

He told me stories of trapping small neighborhood animals—usually raccoons or opossums—throwing them in garbage cans, and dousing them in lighter fluid before tossing in a match and watching them burn. He also told me he stole a friend's pet rat once. Experimented on it for a week before it finally died. I'd give anything to scrub those gory details from my brain, but I'm pretty sure they're permanently embossed in my gray matter.

I don't care how successful or happily married that man is now, there's no getting around his sickness. It's rooted to his core, a living, breathing wickedness that resides deep in his marrow. There's no fixing him, no saving him, and there's certainly no redeeming him.

While I came here to reclaim my life, I also came back to beat him at his own game, to show him he no longer has an ounce of control over me.

I'm in control now.

His life is in *my* hands.

I could ruin him—and I intend to—but only after I draw this out a little longer, make him squirm, bleed his bank accounts dry, and send his wife and children far from his grasp.

He doesn't deserve them.

Delphine rests her chin on her hand, gaze focused on me. Maybe she's replaying our initial meeting in her head, going over all the things I did and didn't divulge.

"How'd you get away?" She frowns.

"I didn't get away so much as I got lucky." Luck has never been a friend of mine, but there's a first time for everything. "One day last summer he showed up, put a cloth sack over my head, and marched me into the woods with a gun shoved into my back. The bastard shot me and left me to die."

"How'd you survive that?" Her mouth is agape.

"He shot me in the shoulder—left side. I think he meant for it to go through my heart, but it missed. Went out the other side. I bled out . . . enough for him to probably think it was a fatal blow. As soon as he was gone, I wrapped my shirt around the wound and sprinted for the nearest clearing. Ended up at some hunter's cabin, where I was able to clean myself up. Cleared out all the man's canned goods when I was done. Ate until I was sick."

I can still taste the salty-sweet tang of cold pork and beans.

"You didn't go to the police?" she asks.

"It's hard to explain the state of mind I was in after all of that . . . survival mode, I guess you could say. I was certain if he knew I was alive, he'd come back and finish the job, so I laid low for as long as I could." I shift in my seat. "In fact, when I was pleading for my life, I promised him I'd stay as good as dead if he let me live. Part of me wonders if he shot me in the shoulder on purpose—if that was his messed-up way of letting me live."

But then that would be assuming there was a kind bone in his body.

There wasn't.

Delphine's lips purse. "So . . . what made you decide to come out of hiding?"

"I was homeless, grifting from town to town, taking jobs no one else wanted because they were the only ones that paid under the table," I say. "Every night, I'd sleep on a park bench or in an alley, and I'd look up at the stars and fantasize about what my life would've been like had I not gotten involved with him in the first place, had I just trusted my gut . . ."

"You can't blame yourself, angel."

"I don't," I say. "It's not about that. I just . . . I want to move on, but I can't. I can't move on until I can get on my feet, and I can't get on my feet until I make some money, and I can't do that without a job. Can't get a job if I'm legally dead—"

Delphine makes her way to my end of the table, wrapping her arms around my shoulders and blanketing me with her earthy-sweet scent. "It's okay. *You're* okay. Everything's going to be okay. One thing at a time."

"And meanwhile, he's living large with his Maserati and his fleet of restaurants," I say. "To watch him with his pregnant wife and to know what he's capable of . . . he doesn't deserve what he has, Delphine. That woman doesn't know what she's sleeping next to every night."

"And how could she?" Delphine asks. "He's a master manipulator."

Maybe I can never force Luca to know the gnawing pain of hunger or to shiver himself to sleep in a drafty cabin, ankles tied and flesh mouse-bitten. But I can level out karma in other ways.

For instance, I have no plans of hurting Merritt or their kids—because I'm not an evil human being, not even close—but I want him to think that I could, to believe I might.

I want him to lose sleep. I want him physically ill with worry. I want his thoughts to be so filled with anguish he doesn't have room to enjoy life's little pleasures. And I want to drain his bank account while

I'm at it—compensation for lost time and wages I'll never recover. But more important than any of that, I want him to know he no longer has an infinitesimal speck of power over me.

His options are slim—which I'm certain is why he's so mum around me, why he's giving me everything I've asked for thus far.

He can't abduct me again. If I go missing, Delphine will point the police straight to him, and it won't be hard for them to connect the dots. And he can't go to the police about the extortion—it'll only invite more questions, and in the end he'll implicate himself.

He can warn Merritt to keep her distance, but he's not with her twenty-four seven. Since he's so busy running his crumbling empire, he doesn't have the freedom that I have. And his funds are running dry—at least according to his own staff—which means his cushy life is being enjoyed on borrowed time . . . and I intend to make that borrowed time as miserable as possible.

CHAPTER
TWENTY-SEVEN

MERRITT

His name is Everett John—it isn't my first choice, but it's what my husband wants, and with all he's been through lately, I decided to let him have that *one* thing. Anything to put a smile on his face again.

The original Everett Coletto—Luca's paternal grandfather—was the one who took him in when he was seventeen, sparing him his last two high school years under his parents' reign of terror. I understand wanting to honor the man for that, but some of the stories I've managed to get out of Luca over the years paint the first Everett in a light that's hardly a shade above flattering.

Still, the human memory has nothing to do with facts and everything to do with emotion.

His grandfather made him feel safe.

Doesn't matter how or why.

"I don't say this to everyone, but you've got a beautiful little boy there," says our nurse, a middle-aged RN named Catherine, as she hovers over our sleeping infant in his hospital bassinet, a grandmother-ish tenderness in her crinkling eyes that reminds me of my mother. I'll never know if having grandchildren would have softened her, but I like to imagine it would've.

I'm sure she *does* say that to everyone—but I appreciate the compliment just the same. Not that I need the confirmation. Our baby is gorgeous with his full head of dark hair, chubby cheeks, and pointed little nose. He's the opposite of Elsie, with her pale hair and rounder features, but they're both perfect in their own ways, head to toe.

"Have you called my sister yet?" I ask Luca when he returns to my recovery suite with takeout bags of breakfast from the cafeteria.

My water broke at three AM. By three thirty, Annette was pulling in the driveway with her overnight bag, and by four, I was checked into the hospital, waiting for the anesthesiologist to start the epidural while the nursing team prepped the OR.

At the time, everything happened in slow motion—and then I blinked and there he was, outside my body, showing off a healthy set of lungs and the kind of hair that'd make Elvis Presley jealous.

In that sliver of a precious moment, nothing else mattered.

Nothing.

"I texted her a picture a little bit ago." He plates my food on a wheeled tray and pushes it over to my bed while the nurse helps me sit up. "She said he's perfect. But we already know that."

He gives me a wink and slides my food closer.

"Have you checked on Elsie?" I ask next. I hate to bark orders, but sitting here connected to wires and monitors with a fresh surgical incision brings out the helplessness in me. Micromanaging gives me some illusion of control, I suppose.

Luca unwraps a breakfast sandwich and takes a seat in a guest chair. "Annette says she's still sleeping, but she'll bring her in once she's up."

I chuckle, knowing what a bear my daughter can be when she doesn't get a solid ten hours of sleep. It's a miracle she didn't wake up in the midst of all the middle-of-the-night chaos, but we managed to make it out without a stir.

"I'll be back to check on you in about an hour." Catherine peeks at her watch as someone pages her over the intercom around her neck. "Buzz me if you need anything."

When she's gone, Luca scoots his chair to my bedside.

There's a lightness, in this moment. A catharsis of sorts. As if everything we'd ever wanted was dumped into a few short hours. But that release is short-lived. While we have our daughter and our son and each other, the moment we leave this hospital three days from now, we're going to walk right back into the mess with Lydia.

Luca would be upset if he knew I still worry, that his comforting words only ever quell my concerns for a short moment. They always return stronger than before, that niggling voice in the back of my mind telling me there's nothing my husband can say or do to prevent the other shoe from dropping.

The deepest part of me fears it's not a matter of if . . . but when.

His phone chimes on the bedside table. He grabs it in record time. This isn't normal Luca behavior. This isn't the husband I know.

"Who is it?" I force a nonchalant innocence into my voice.

He darkens the screen and slides the phone into his back pocket. "Just the restaurant. Had a question about an order that came in this morning."

It's believable *enough* under ordinary circumstances.

I don't buy it. I try. But I can't. My throat swells, and the food turns to rocks in my stomach. Maybe it's the pain medicine or the whirlwind several hours that have just happened, but my body is rebelling against *something*.

"What are you not telling me?" My mouth is bone dry. I'd reach for my water, but my fingers tremble so hard I'd likely drop it. "Ever since Lydia came back, you've been distant. And whenever I try to talk to you about it, you smooth it over or change the subject or tell me not to worry. And then you make decisions without me."

He doesn't speak. Doesn't chew. Doesn't protest. Doesn't move.

"I'm tired of pretending everything's going to be fine," I say. "We need to get real, or you're going to lose me. You're going to lose *us*."

I've never threatened him before—I've never needed to.

But these are unprecedented times.

A full breath lifts his posture. Placing the remnants of his meal aside, he hunches over the edge of my bed, sliding his hand over mine. When he meets my stare, his dark eyes are glassy and brimming with tears.

In all the years I've known this man, he hasn't shed a single tear. Not once.

"Let me have this day." His words are a broken whisper, and in this moment, I'm reminded of the man he was when we first met.

Before I respond, he rises and moves for the bassinet, sweeping our newborn son into his arms, his back toward me. The sunlight filtering through the parking-lot-view window engulfs them in a picture-perfect veil of light.

But still, I can't help but wonder—does he want this day?

Or does he want more time to figure out what he's going to tell me?

CHAPTER
TWENTY-EIGHT

LYDIA

"You can't work for that man anymore," Delphine tells me after I fill her in on everything. For two hours, she listened in silence. Nodding. Wincing. Gasping. Hands clasped. At one point, she went outside for fresh air and a breather. And when she returned, she sat back down and motioned for me to continue. When it was over, I insisted she google me and encouraged her to fact-check any and everything she felt necessary.

Of course, I can't prove nine years of torture beyond the marks on my body . . .

"If what he did to you is true," she adds, "you're not safe. And I realize I'm not your mother, and you're a grown woman. I can't forbid you from doing anything or seeing anyone. But I also cannot, in good faith, let you set foot over there again."

"I don't expect you to understand any of—"

She slices a hand through the air, her bracelets clanging. "You don't fight evil with evil."

But if I don't, who will?

Seeing that man in handcuffs serving a measly twenty years for kidnapping and attempted murder would be a slap on the wrist compared to the hell he put me through. And knowing his luck, he'd be out in fifteen for good behavior.

"All due respect, I'd hardly call myself evil," I say.

"That may be true," she says, her clear blue eyes wilder than usual. "But you don't fight fire with fire . . . that only makes more fire."

"So I should kill him with kindness?" I sniff. I'm pretty sure I've been more than kind to him by not going to the police the first chance I had.

"Use the proper channels," she says, smacking the tabletop. "Go to the authorities, tell them who you are and what happened, and let them handle him. Then and only then can you get your identity back."

I rise from the table and help myself to another glass of tap water for my parched throat. I can't recall a single incident in my life when anyone listened to me talk for hours.

"He's slippery," I say. "He'd weasel his way out of this. Put a second mortgage on his house to hire a lawyer, find a loophole, and walk away unscathed. Plus, I don't doubt he'd try to finish the job should he get the chance. Once an opportunist, always an opportunist. In any scenario where Luca's walking around a free man, I might as well be walking around a dead woman. Again."

"You don't know that."

"I have it on good authority he's currently liquidating," I say. "And why would someone liquidate a lucrative business empire if they weren't planning on skipping town? He knows I can go to the police at any time . . . he's getting his ducks in a row."

"People have all kinds of reasons . . ."

"I'm not exactly in a position to give him the benefit of the doubt."

Leaning back in her seat, she raps her knuckles against the table. "This doesn't have to be as hard as you're making it, Lydia."

I keep my back to her. I adore this woman, but she doesn't get it. And how can she? She hasn't lived through an ounce of what I have. I'm sorry she married a closeted gay man and that her daughter got caught up with the wrong crowd, but she doesn't get to tell me I've made my life harder than it has to be.

I endured nine years at the hand of the devil himself.

I nearly bled to death on the earthen ground of a forest miles from civilization or help.

For six months, I lived under the radar. I shoveled literal pig shit in exchange for under-the-table pay that amounted to half the minimum wage. I collected cans from the side of the highway until I had enough for a fifty-cent gas station snack cake—which was occasionally the only thing I'd eat for days. I fielded suspicious questions from police who were certain I was walking the streets in search of johns, drugs, or both. I slept in the rain and cold. I drank from creeks. I bathed in the ocean.

But the hardest thing I ever did . . . was walk up to Luca's door.

As far as I'm concerned, it's all downhill from here.

I've come too far to take the high road, to let him *win*.

"You've lost an entire decade of your life because of him," she says. "Why give him another second of your attention? He probably likes it. Deep down, he's probably getting off on seeing you again."

She doesn't know Luca like I do. That's not how he works. She hasn't seen the silent panic in his eyes as he tries to stifle his reactions in my presence. She doesn't know that his frozen demeanor is nothing more than a mask to disguise his crumbling interior.

My being here terrifies him.

And maybe not in the same way he terrified me.

But terror is terror.

"I'm not saying you should forgive and forget," she continues. "But maybe consider going to the police and letting him be someone else's problem so you can focus on yourself. Don't give him another minute of your life. He's already taken so much."

My phone vibrates. I flip it open to find a small, grainy picture of a swaddled infant with pitch-black hair.

"What is it?" Delphine asks.

"Luca's wife just texted me a picture of their baby," I say.

"She thinks you're friends, doesn't she?" Delphine asks. "All this time you've been spending with her."

"I think she's scared I'm going to take Luca from her, and this is her way of begging for me not to break up her happy home. If she only knew . . ."

I fold the phone and toss it on the counter, cupping my hands over my nose and mouth and exhaling.

Delphine comes to my side, placing a palm gently on my arm. "It's okay if you like her, Lydia. She's not the one who hurt you."

"This is probably one of the best days of her life," I say. "He's probably sitting right next to her, and she has no idea who he really is. *What* he really is."

"Or maybe she does." Delphine lifts a shoulder to her ear.

I lean against the counter, replaying various conversations I've had with Merritt over the weeks and the way her pretty face lights in Luca's presence. Nothing that's come out of her mouth has given me any indication that there's more than meets the eye or that she's aware of her husband's sadistic side. She's a typical vapid, materialistic, West Coast housewife trying desperately to maintain her cushy lifestyle and picture-perfect family.

That said, I don't resent her.

None of this is her fault.

"Maybe when this is over, the two of you can be friends," Delphine says. "Real friends. Once the dust settles, I mean. If you value your relationship with her, write her back. Tell her the baby is beautiful, that sort of thing. Leave any mention of Luca out of it."

"And then what?" I envision the police storming her hospital room, leaving with her handcuffed husband, her newborn screaming, some detective filling her in. Premature sympathetic betrayal sours my mouth.

It's probably best I ignore it. I can't, in good faith, send her a sweet message knowing I'm on the verge of tearing down her entire world. Besides, I don't think there'll come a day when we'll ever be friends, even if Luca's behind bars. There's too much baggage to unpack. Too many intricacies. We'll look at each other and only see him. He'll color every facet of that friendship. The constant undercurrent.

After this, I need to move on.

"I don't know, angel." Delphine rubs my back, and for the first time, I don't recoil. Not even a little. "Wait right here, will you?"

Grabbing her shop keys off the counter, she disappears downstairs before returning a few minutes later with a small beaded necklace in hand.

"You're going to think I'm silly," she says with a half laugh. "And I'm sure you already do. I can tell you're not into this stuff . . . but I'd feel better if you'd wear this."

Seven polished, bead-sized stones strung on a gold chain rest in her palm, finished with a metal clasp.

"It's for protection." She massages the stones one by one between her thumb and forefinger. "Bloodstone, red jasper, black tourmaline, white howlite, tiger's eye, moonstone, and smoky quartz. These are the big ones. Will you wear this?" Her pale brows raise. "For me?"

The rocks are small, the necklace unobtrusive enough.

I certainly can't imagine it'd make anything *worse* . . .

"Sure." I lift my hair, turn, and let her secure it. It's lighter than I expected, the beads smooth and cool against my hot flesh. "Thank you."

Her warm palms rest on my shoulders as she whispers words so slight I can't hear them. A quiet prayer, perhaps. Something to soothe her own nerves.

"Please think about what I said . . . about going to the police." She lets me go. "Sleep on it if you have to. I just . . . I have a terrible feeling." When I turn back, I find her clutching at her stomach, her hands balled into tight fists. "You might think you have the upper hand in this situation, but it's only because he's letting you think that."

My blood turns to ice with her words.

CHAPTER
TWENTY-NINE

MERRITT

The baby doesn't sleep.

Sometime in the middle of the night, he decided to stop latching. It always starts with the same agonizing screams, his little face turning plum purple and bloodred. Sooner or later a nurse rushes in to save the day, insisting I send him to the nursery so I can rest and assuring me that a couple of Similacs here or there aren't going to sabotage my breastfeeding efforts.

The instant they wheeled him away, I was flooded with a cocktail of guilt and relief with a pain garnish thanks to my incision.

I don't remember Elsie being this fussy. We had our little health scare with her in the beginning, but after that she was content, as if she were simply happy to be here. Everett doesn't seem to want to be here at all . . .

The clock above the TV reads 2:34 AM. Luca sleeps soundly on the foldout guest couch in the corner. At least I think he's sleeping. It's hard to know from over here, alone in my rock-hard hospital bed, too helpless to reach my water jug.

I texted Lydia a picture of the baby two days ago.

No response.

Yet another concern to add to the pile . . .

Tomorrow morning we'll be discharged. The last few days have lacked an undercurrent of tenderness that should accompany these life moments. And Luca's quietude has only magnified that. When Elsie was born, he called everyone he knew. He talked nonstop, manic almost. He sang to her. He came *alive*.

With Everett, he's merely going through the motions.

He's here, but he's also a world away.

I need my husband back—the man he was before, the man I know he can be again.

CHAPTER THIRTY

LYDIA

The parking lot of *sea bats* is vacant Monday morning—save for the sous chef's hybrid Honda, random Lexus, and Luca's glossy Maserati.

I spent all weekend digesting Delphine's advice, waxing and waning and changing my mind every five seconds. Some moments, I was overwhelmed with a sense of calm, certain that Delphine's path was the right choice. Other times, that calm would be overridden with a burst of anger so hot my skin burned from the inside out. I promised myself I'd reach a decision by Sunday night—and now I'm here . . . but only because Luca still owes me two thousand from last Thursday and Friday, and I'm not about to let him skip out on that.

After he ponies up, I should have enough for an apartment deposit, some furniture, and a little something extra. It isn't as much as I'd hoped to glean from the bastard, but after talking to Delphine over the weekend, I've decided to go to the police sooner than later. No sense in drawing this out or staying on his level any longer than necessary. All I'm doing is giving him more time to plan his escape.

I jam my master key into the back door and head in, passing my locked office and heading straight for his. The door is open halfway, a desk lamp spilling a triangular shape of light that stops just short of the jamb.

Steeling myself, I offer a loud, "Welcome back."

He jolts. Not a lot, but enough to show he wasn't expecting me. A week ago, I'd have laughed about it, but now Delphine's words ring in my ears, and I can't help but wonder if it's all an act. The Luca *I* knew was never this jumpy. He'd have never rolled over and taken *any* of this.

There's a definite possibility I'm being played like a goddamned fiddle, that the joke is on me.

Again.

"I know you've been busy having a baby and all, but I couldn't help but notice the lack of funds on my desk last week." I slide my hands in my back pockets, an irritatingly casual move, I'm sure. But I don't want to tip him off that anything has changed on my end. As far as he knows, as long as he keeps shoving money at me, I'm keeping my lips sealed. "I'm short two grand."

He gives me a death stare before sliding a drawer out, retrieving a thick manila envelope, and dropping it on the desktop.

I retrieve the cash and step back a couple of feet, not wanting to be closer to him than necessary.

"How much longer do you plan to extort me?" he asks, hovering over his mouse and shutting down his computer. It's barely nine AM. He had to have just gotten here . . .

The wrinkled-polo-and-jeans outfit he's sporting is a far cry from his usual designer-suit-and-tie ensemble. He's on his way out. The only question: Where is he going?

"I don't enjoy being in your life any more than you enjoy me being in it," I say, giving him a roundabout answer.

He clicks off his marble-and-brass banker's lamp.

"Leaving already?" I move toward the doorway, planting myself just outside the frame. Beyond his office window, the sky is almost as dark as night as another storm system rolls through.

"I'm going home to be with Merritt and the baby." He makes his way to the front of his desk, then toward me. I step farther into the hall, and he tugs the door closed before sliding his key into the lock. Oddly enough, he doesn't turn it. Maybe it's exhaustion, maybe it's the distraction of being in such close proximity to me, but he forgets to secure it. "I'll have everything else for you soon."

"Everything else?" I ask.

"The things you asked for last week . . ."

Ah, yes. The new identity.

"I'm also working on getting you a car. Something reliable. If I give you those things, will you leave us alone?" His coffee-brown irises dare to meet mine, intensified by the matching dark circles beneath his eyes. He's a case study in fatigue—mental, physical, emotional. If those things are even possible for a sociopath to feel. For the first time, I *almost* feel sorry for him. But I could never. "You're getting your life back. And this one's arguably better than the one you had before."

"Debatable," I interject.

That's not for him to decide.

"You're bleeding me dry, you're worrying my wife sick, you've tainted the birth of my second child with your petty bullshit games. I'm giving you *everything* you asked for—what more do you want?"

"Whoa, whoa, whoa." I lift a palm and give an incredulous snort, keeping any hint of a smile at bay. Not sure whom he thinks he's kidding or what alternate reality he's stepped into. "Are you actually playing the victim here? Because I'm pretty sure you weren't the one tortured and raped and starved and threatened for nine years of your life."

Pots and pans clang from the kitchen. Whoever's in there is far from earshot, but it's a reminder we're not alone.

Luca lowers his chin. "This isn't the time or the place, Lydia."

"Then name the time and the place, and I'll be there. We're having this conversation, we're correcting this course. I'm not leaving until you make this right."

"What the hell do you think I'm trying to do?" Spittle leaves his lips as he keeps his tone hushed. He closes the distance between us so tight I can smell his morning coffee. "What more do you want from me, Lydia?"

I want to see him suffer. Maybe not in the physical, vile ways I suffered. But he doesn't get to buy my silence and ride off into the sunset with his stock-photo family. Monsters aren't supposed to get happy endings.

My phone vibrates in my pocket—perhaps Delphine's wondering where I ran off to this morning. I haven't told her what I decided yet. I'm sure she's freaking out—whatever that looks like for a tranquil person.

But that's when it hits me—most phones have record features.

If I can get him alone, get him talking about what happened . . . I could present it to the police. They'd have no reason not to take me seriously and every reason to mark him as a dangerous criminal, doing everything in their power to get him into custody before he could hurt another person. At least, I assume.

It's worth a shot.

"I'm going to have to ask for your patience," he says in a voice too passive to be coming from a monster. "I'm going to be gone these next couple of weeks."

"What, why?" I squint. "Your wife literally had a baby four days ago."

I don't have experience around new mothers, but I can't imagine someone wanting to spend those first weeks on vacation.

"Exactly," he says. "She's struggling a bit, and I'm going to spend the next two weeks helping out."

"How noble of you."

Luca rolls his eyes.

"I thought you had a nanny?" I ask.

"The nanny's for our daughter." He shoves his keys in his pocket and eyes the nearest exit. "Please, Lydia. You don't owe me a damn thing, but give us these two weeks. After that, I'll give you anything you want."

I imagine Merritt at home, tired and sore, walking around in a sleepless stupor. I've yet to text her back from last week. A day had passed, then another.

I should know better than to accept a promise from this man, but he's already out the door before I have a chance to offer a rebuttal. A second later, his Maserati growls to life and he peels out of the parking lot, taillights disappearing into the distance.

Heart pulsing in my ears, I press on his door handle . . . and it swings open. Taking a quick look around the restaurant, I make sure I'm in the clear before heading in. I close the door and leave the lights off.

I'm not sure what I'm looking for, I just know what opportunity looks like.

A shelf mounted on the far wall houses a myriad of pictures—Luca and Merritt enjoying a picnic, Luca and his daughter at the zoo, the three of them swinging at a park, Merritt in some kind of artsy maternity shoot with draping fabric and a glowing grin. A wedding photo complete with Hawaiian leis and a volcano in the background. Given what I know of his parents and what she's told me about hers, eloping to some exotic destination fits.

I take a seat in his desk chair, which creaks despite my minuscule size, and I glance toward the door to ensure no one comes to investigate. A second later, I slide open the top drawer, the one that held my envelope of money, only to find it filled with meticulously organized office supplies. Staple refills. Gel pens—all blue. Yellow Post-its. Wite-Out. Silver paper clips. Nothing stands out. Pushing it closed, I move for the second drawer, this one filled with various computer cords and a phone charger. The bottom drawer—a file cabinet—is locked.

I rifle through the top drawer again in search of a key.

Nothing.

Running my palm around the underside of his desktop, I feel around until my fingers touch metal. Dropping to my knees, I examine my find—only to discover it's a piece of desk hardware. A hinge connecting the top to the cabinet piece.

Determined, I continue my quest for twenty minutes, using my dim phone screen as a makeshift flashlight and examining every crevice and corner of this office. My knees throb and my back aches when I'm finished, but I refuse to give up this easily. Grabbing a paper clip from the first drawer, I unfold it and jam it into the lock, twisting and contorting it until it catches on something—a fruitless five-minute waste of my time. In a last-ditch attempt to access whatever's hiding behind this faux wooden facade, I press my work key into the lock . . . and it slides in with ease.

"Holy shit." I clap my hand over my mouth when the internal mechanism gives and the file drawer glides open. Presented before me in meticulous order is an array of various manila file folders with printed labels, all alphabetized.

I scan each one—accounting, back room stock, chef applicants, deliveries, *estate*.

One of these things is not like the others.

I slide the estate file out of its holder and push myself up. Flipping it open, I page through it like a book, ensuring I keep the loose pages in order. Nothing stands out at first. There's a notarized will and testament. An old 401(k) report. A copy of a mortgage statement. An envelope with a key to a safe-deposit box at Bent Creek National Bank. A handful of savings bonds.

I flick to the next page, and the next. Halting when I find a document with my name on it. The words OFFICIAL RECORD OF MARRIAGE line the top of a heat-sensitive paper, along with an embossed stamp. Our old marriage certificate.

Folding it in half, I slide it into my cash envelope—it's mine now, and I have every intention of setting it on fire the first chance I get. But for now I move to the next item: a life insurance declaration page.

Policy Number: A83GW-282
Insured: Lydia Ellen Coletto
Age: Twenty
Sex: F
Premium Class: Preferred-Term
Owner: Luca Coletto
Beneficiary: Luca Coletto
Amount of Insurance: $2 million for twenty years

The walls close in around me as I forget to breathe.

Oh, my God.

It makes sense now . . .

His marriage to me wasn't just a way to fulfill his sick and twisted fantasies. It was also a way to profit off my death—which is how he funded his restaurants, landed his beautiful wife, and ricocheted to the moon with the life of his dreams. A brisk chill zips down my spine, but I shake it off. I'll have to process this later.

Stuffing my nausea down, I fold the document in half and place it with the marriage license before returning to the folder. The next document is just as concerning.

Policy Number: A34YW-991
Insured: Merritt Sylvia Coletto
Age: Forty-one
Sex: F
Premium Class: Preferred-Term
Owner: Luca Coletto
Beneficiary: Luca Coletto
Amount of Insurance: $4 million for twenty years

Oh, my God.

When I flip to the next document, I'm met with another policy declaration page, this one for his daughter, Elsabeth, for $1 million. I try to wrap my head around any scenario in which a small child would require a million-dollar life insurance policy . . .

Only one comes to mind.

CHAPTER THIRTY-ONE

MERRITT

"Everything okay at the restaurant?" I stumble through the kitchen in a sleepless daze, heading straight for the coffee maker before I remember I'm breastfeeding. Or at least trying to. We've been home all of one day, and it's still not going well.

"Of course." Luca drops his car keys on the counter, studying me. "Where's the baby?"

"Sleeping." I yawn. My incision throbs. I need to slow down, but as exhausted as I am, I can't bring myself to sit still. There's always a task to do, a thought to think. "For now."

"You should lie down."

"That's the plan." I give him a sleepy wink, trying to keep things light so as to distract from any residual resentment in my tone. "Was waiting for you to get home . . ."

"What do you say we get out of town for a bit? Maybe go to Willow Branch for a week or two?"

If I had a mouthful of coffee, I'd have spat it out by now. "We have a four-day-old baby, and you want to go to Willow Branch?"

We haven't been to our farmhouse getaway since last summer. It's probably freezing there, and in desperate need of a good cleaning and airing out. Not the ideal place to take a newborn. Plus the thought of riding two hours in a car with a colicky infant . . .

Luca strolls up to me, cool and steady, and cups my bare face in his hands. For a second, he looks at me the way he used to—like I was the prettiest, most splendid thing he'd ever seen in his life. The fact that I'm sporting unwashed hair and smell like spit-up makes me wonder if he was acting all those times before. I couldn't be more opposite of splendid.

"He has his mother—that's all he needs," Luca says, voice as smooth as velvet. "Fresh air and a change of scenery could be good for us all, don't you think?"

I study his face.

"Did something happen?" I swallow. "With Lydia?"

"No." His brows angle. "Nothing happened. But I don't think a precaution would be the worst thing we could do."

"You think she's going to do something to us? To the baby?" I ask. "I texted her last week, told her we'd had the baby. I was trying to be friendly. I mean, I thought we were friends. She still hasn't texted back. Maybe it set her off?"

"Mer." He captures my hands in his. "Slow down. *Calm* down. Don't jump to conclusions. Like I said, change of scenery. Fresh air. And a little distance from everything going on. I think it'd be good for us."

The farmhouse in the summertime is a sight for sore eyes. Surrounded by ancient leafy oaks, accented with a docked fishing pond, and neighboring a pasture filled with dappled Appaloosas, it's a country lover's paradise. But this time of year, it's brown and bleak as far as the eye can see.

"We can start with a few days and go from there," he says. "I told *sea bats* I'd be gone for two weeks. They'll be fine without me."

"You trust Lydia there?" A getaway with a newborn isn't conventional, but fresh air . . . and distance . . . might be exactly what we need to turn this ship around. All we need is a bassinet and the basics—bottles, blankets, diapers. Anything we forget, we can get at the store in town.

"She sits in an office all day messing around on an old computer I set up," he says with a smirk. "There's nothing she can do. I put the head chef in charge. He'll call me if anything comes up."

Leaning in, he presses a tender kiss against my chapped lips, lingering longer than he has in forever.

"Go lie down." He escorts me to our room, his hand on the small of my back. "We can pack after you've had some rest, and we'll leave tonight."

I'm not sure I have the energy to pack, but I'll scrape it from the depths of my wearied soul if I have to.

He's coming back to me—fragment by fragment. There's life in his voice again. An extra beat of energy in his step.

This is the man I know.

This is the man I love.

He never left; he was just buried under a mountain of stress.

Luca helps me settle into bed before pulling the shades. The room is dark, but not enough to block out all the daylight. My frenzied mind conjures up list after list of all the things I'll need to pack, not just for the baby, but for Elsie, myself, and Luca, too. I always pack for him. If I don't, he'll end up forgetting underwear or toothpaste.

My husband is a big-picture guy.

I'm better at remembering the little things.

My incision pulses with a red-hot pain that dulls to a subtle ache. I'm supposed to go in for a follow-up later this week so they can remove the staples, but I'm sure there's a doctor in Willow Branch who can squeeze me in. Whatever we have to do, we'll make this work.

I stare at the lifeless ceiling fan until I can't take it any longer. Hauling myself out of bed, I shuffle to the walk-in closet, grab our luggage, and start packing for our little adventure.

CHAPTER
THIRTY-TWO

LYDIA

"Can I help you?" A college-aged receptionist greets me in the front of the Brian Hoffmeier Insurance Agency in downtown Bent Creek Monday afternoon.

Canned music pipes from speakers in the ceiling, and the chairs in the waiting room make my back hurt just looking at them. A fake potted tree, magazine rack, and water cooler complete the look.

"Hi." I step closer to her, shoving my manila packet under my arm and tucking my hands in my pockets to hide their fidgeting. "Is Brian available?"

"Do you have an appointment?" She cradles the reception phone on her shoulder.

"No, actually. I was just hoping I could have a minute of his time?"

Her round eyes drag the length of me. She's probably wondering if I'm selling something—magazine subscriptions or religion or something. This town is full of those types.

"I have some questions about a life insurance policy he sold." I wave the packet. "I'll be superquick, I promise."

Her overplucked brows meet and she double-clicks her computer mouse, squinting at the screen. "His next appointment should be here any minute . . ."

"Two minutes," I say with a friendly smile.

She tucks a strand of bleached-blonde hair behind one ear before punching in a couple of numbers and mumbling something into the phone.

"He'll be out in a sec," she says. "Feel free to have a seat."

Five minutes later, a fortysomething man with a garage-gym body and thinning silver hair steps into the waiting area, rubbing his hands together like a coach about to go over a football play.

"You must be the young lady with the quick question?" he asks with a wholesome chuckle. A gold cross necklace hangs from his neck, peeking out from his insurance-logo'd polo. "Come on back. I've only got a few minutes, but let's see what we can do for you."

He closes the office door behind us and folds himself into his desk chair while I pull the declaration pages out of my envelope, ensuring I don't spill any cash in the process.

Glancing over the top page, he chews the inside of his lip. "This looks like an old policy . . . yeah . . . this one expired about seven, eight years ago. At least according to this declaration page."

"Was it cashed out?" I ask despite knowing the answer.

"I'm afraid I can only disclose that to the policy holder." He leans over the page again. "Luca Coletto. Ah, yes. I know Mr. Coletto. Nice man."

Hardly.

"Sorry to hear about his first wife. What a tragedy," he adds.

I don't tell him he's looking at her.

"So can *anyone* get a two-million-dollar life insurance policy on someone else?" I ask.

His hands fold into a temple near his lips as he studies me. "In theory, yes. Certain underwriters require specific thresholds or have different requirements. For instance, someone making twenty grand a year can't go out and get a five-million-dollar policy. Too big of a spread. Tends to be a red flag—especially if it's not someone's spouse or domestic partner. Of course there are always exceptions. Just depends on the company. Open market varies quite a bit. Always changing."

"So wouldn't a two-million-dollar policy on a small-town waitress be a red flag?" I ask.

"Could be," he says. "Depends on the other factors. If they're married, some insurers will disregard that."

"What if they've only been married a short time?" I ask.

He offers a strained smile, like he's trying to be polite despite his confusion. "Lots of variables in these situations and not nearly enough time to go over them. Besides, I'm afraid I only sell the policies—I don't underwrite them."

"How long does someone have to be dead before you can file a claim on their policy?" I ask my next question knowing our time together is dwindling by the second.

"Most people file a claim within thirty days of getting a death certificate," he says. "Not everyone, but I'd say the majority do. Tends to be paid out fairly quickly. Considered nontaxable income."

"What's a policy like this cost?" I ask next.

He frowns. "Again, lots of variables. Depends on the agency, the company paying out, the health of the insured, that sort of thing."

"What if it's someone young and healthy?" I point to my name on the page. "Like a twenty-year-old?"

"Those tend to be more affordable," he says. "Two, maybe three thousand for a policy of this size? At the most? And if we're talking ten years ago, could be considerably less. Hard to say. Depends on the physical, too."

"What if there was no physical?"

"That's rare, but it happens. Those kinds of policies tend to cost a little more than average."

I was taken in July, a week after Independence Day. By late August, the search efforts were officially called off after authorities declared they'd done all they could. Within four years, Luca had filed a case with the local courts to have me legally declared dead, and it took another year to finalize it after all the formalities. Lots of hoops to jump through, but a clean two million would be enough to motivate the laziest of individuals to stay the course.

Brian's desk phone rings, and he offers me an apologetic wince before taking the call. When he hangs up, he rises. "I'm so sorry, miss. My next appointment's here. Did I answer all your questions?"

"You did." I gather my papers and return them to my envelope, maintaining their pristine condition despite my haste. "Thanks for your time."

Heading out, I think of the summer Luca took me. Our rusting car with the noisy muffler. Our perpetually stained and faded clothes. The way he'd sometimes spend his lunch breaks looking for loose change in parking lots.

To call us dirt poor would've been an understatement—and he wasn't exactly rolling in dough when he worked at the diner in Greenbrook either. It would have been impossible for him to scrounge up a couple of grand to cover a life insurance policy—unless he'd been saving and planning for years.

I'm halfway to Delphine's when my phone buzzes with a text . . . from Luca.

Speak of the devil.

It's a set of coordinates, but seeing how my phone has no internet browser or navigation, I can't exactly pull it up.

A second message comes through a few seconds later: For your fresh start.

I wait for another message, maybe something with details? But my phone stays silent.

If he bought me someone's identity, it's not like he can spell it out. He can't write, "Go here for your new Social Security Number." Anyone with half a brain cell would be cryptic about this sort of thing.

But still—I don't trust him.

I shove my phone into my pocket and keep walking.

It'd be tempting to grab my new name and bag of cash and skip town, heading somewhere this lunatic could never find me, but the declaration pages in my envelope are singing a different tune. If he's capable of doing that to me, what's to stop him from doing that to his new family?

I take the long way home and use the extra time to devise a new plan.

CHAPTER
THIRTY-THREE

MERRITT

It's dark when we get to the farmhouse, and in the full moonlight, the wintry oak trees appear more skeletal than ever. But it's our home away from home, and we're going to make the most of it. Two hours east of Bent Creek, there's no way Lydia can bother us here.

The shadow of my husband's past doesn't reach this far.

I pull a chilly breath into my lungs when we step out, my sneaker scuffing against the gravel driveway. Luca tosses me the keys and retrieves a sleeping Elsie from the back seat, propping her on his hip before unsnapping the infant carrier from its base.

I never understood what he saw in this place—at least not at first. It was isolating and depressing. An estate sale. Some middle-aged off-spring unloading their family farm for a cool seven-hundred-fifty grand split three ways. Just like that, a legacy ended.

We must have toured the place half a dozen times before Luca sold me on it, saying it'd be a great escape from the coast. A place to bring our future children. Sure we had trees and water in Bent Creek, but these were deciduous trees, not evergreens. And we didn't have a private fishing pond to paddleboat around in. He painted the most captivating picture of how things could be for us out here. Giggling children chasing fireflies. Feeding carrots to the neighbor's horses. Hitting up the farmer's market on Saturday. No one to impress with our expensive cars.

We could breathe out here, he said. And he was right. The coast is exciting and fast-paced, but it can be suffocating at times.

The house is an invigorating fifty-eight degrees inside since we keep it just warm enough to prevent the pipes from bursting should there be an unexpected cold snap. I head for the thermostat, nudging it up to seventy-four as if that could heat the place any faster, and Luca carries Elsie to the toddler bed in the spare bedroom.

I flick on the kitchen lights next, scanning the decades-old oaky decor and checking the cabinets to make sure we haven't acquired any rodent friends since our time here last summer. I check the fridge, a humming Maytag beast with a broken ice maker, next and find a moldy block of Gruyère and a bottle of pinot in the door.

Grabbing a pen and notepad from the junk drawer, I take a seat at the rickety kitchen table and scribble down a grocery list. My incision burns, but only for a second. Last I knew, the local grocery doesn't offer online ordering, and I don't think I have the stamina for running errands yet. Maybe I can sweet-talk them into doing a phone order. A little kindness goes a long way, especially in Willow Branch, where it's practically a second form of currency.

I fasten the list to the fridge with a John Deere magnet and trek to the living room, where Luca has left a sleeping Everett in his car seat. I tuck his downy-soft blanket around him before lowering myself into a nearby recliner. An old grandfather clock in the hall ticks, echoing off the walls as I wait for my husband to return from Elsie's room.

Enough light spills in from outside to illuminate the wood-burning fireplace on the north wall, as well as the built-in shelves that house an assortment of family-friendly DVDs and timeless board games—all of which were left by the previous owners. A full warmth gushes through my body as I envision a time in our lives when our babies are older and we can sit around making memories. I even go so far as to imagine a decades-from-now era when our grandchildren will visit in the summertime.

Who needs a French chateau or house in the Hamptons when you have all this space? All this peace? All this serenity? And a mere two hours away, if that.

"Found some extra blankets in the hall closet." Luca appears at the bottom of the stairs. I'd been so lost in thought I hadn't heard him come down. "Elsie should stay warm until the heat kicks on."

"Could you bring the bassinet in from the car and put it in the master?" I shouldn't call it a master bedroom. It's simply the biggest of the three rooms upstairs. There's no en suite, no walk-in closet. It's hardly spacious enough for a queen-sized bed, two nightstands, and a chest of drawers. But while it may not have a million-dollar view, we can see the pond and the big red barn from our windows. The summer sunrises here are a sight for sore eyes.

Without a word, Luca heads outside with careful steps so as not to wake Everett, and I settle into the chair, brushing my cheek against its soft, aging microfiber before closing my eyes.

I couldn't sleep on the drive here. Too much excitement, perhaps? The forecast for this week is bleak and chilly, but it's supposed to warm up next Saturday. I picture myself rocking the baby on the wraparound porch next weekend while Elsie and her father run around in the yard. Coats and gloves and a million blankets, of course, but carefree smiles all around.

And not a care in the world.

I jerk myself awake—with no idea how long I've been out. I don't even remember falling asleep. Sitting up, I check on Everett in the car seat . . . but he's gone. Luca must have taken him to bed. A blanket falls from my lap when I push myself up—yet another thoughtful Luca move.

We haven't spent a single night in this house, but already things are looking up.

By the time I make my way upstairs, the burning ache along my lower abdomen reminds me I'm due for another pain pill—but I don't have the energy to trudge downstairs, nor do I want to wake my husband, so I suffer through it. Besides, Everett should be up soon for another feeding.

I use these still, quiet minutes to watch my husband dream with the most peaceful expression painted on his handsome face. With heavy eyelids and a weary half smile on my lips, I succumb to a wave of blissful exhaustion and allow my body—and mind—to rest.

Lord knows I need it.

"I'm sorry, ma'am, the card didn't go through. Is there another you can try?" the chipper young grocery associate informs me from the other end of the phone the next morning. I'd called the Willow Branch Market, played the sleep-deprived-new-mother card with the store manager, and arranged for them to shop my order and have it ready for Luca to pick up within the hour.

"Are you sure?" I ask. "Try it again."

Silence. Then a jarring electronic beep.

"If you want, we can try another card?" he asks.

"Are your machines down?" Internet in rural Oregon can be shoddy.

He clears his throat. "No, ma'am."

Swiping my purse off the counter, I rummage for my wallet, pulling out a black Visa and rattling off the numbers.

"I'm sorry, ma'am. This one was declined," he says after an endless minute.

"There's got to be some kind of mistake." Last I checked there were thousands of dollars in my personal checking account. And the Visa has an exceedingly high limit, given our status as preferred customers.

"The first one just said transaction failed, but this last one actually said declined," he says. "Maybe we can try a different card?"

I pitch the black Visa across the counter and grab a bright-orange Discover from a side pocket. It's for emergencies only, and I can't remember the last time I used this one. In fact, I don't even think Luca knows I have it.

"Okay," he says, his voice perkier than a minute ago. "That one went through. We should have your order ready for pickup by eight thirty."

I thank the poor kid and end the call. Hunched over the counter, I retrieve the pieces of plastic I'd thrown in a fit of frustration and call the numbers on the back to check the balances.

"Your checking account balance is . . . zero . . . dollars," a computerized voice tells me. Heat creeps up my skin when I hang up and call Visa. A minute later, their system tells me I'm eight dollars and twenty-two cents over my limit, and that the last five transactions were cash withdrawals in thousand-dollar chunks.

Have we been hacked?

Is Lydia behind this?

Or is our financial situation worse than I've been told, and Luca's scraping the bottom of every barrel we have?

My lower stomach stings with each step as I march to the living room, where my husband and babies are spread out on a blanket, surrounded by soft books, stuffed animals, and plastic blocks.

"You okay?" His thick brows lift when he spots me bracing myself against the doorway.

Swallowing a painful breath, I unclench my jaw. "I'm tired of being in the dark. It ends now."

His dark eyes track me, and he pushes himself up from the blanket, laughing almost. "What?"

I speak through gritted teeth. "Tell me *everything*."

"What are you talking about?" His hands rest on his hips, cool and casual. Insulting. "Tell you what exactly?"

"All the things you're not telling me," I elaborate. "I want to know. Money, Lydia . . . like I said—*everything*."

I follow him to the foyer.

"Things aren't good," he says, pacing.

I've half a mind to grab him by the shoulders and nail him to the wall until he stops moving. All this back and forth is dizzying.

"Heard back from the last buyer a few days ago." He pinches the bridge of his nose. "They passed. All of them did."

"What? When were you going to tell me this?"

He frowns. "Not while you were in the hospital . . ."

"Why'd they pass?" The sting of rejection is personal with this one. While the restaurants were a joint effort, I'm the one who chose every menu item, the fabric on the drapes, the light fixtures, the music. The entire experience—from the moment a diner walks in to the second they return to the parking lot, belly swollen with unforgettable cuisine and veins flooded with top-shelf liquor—was all me. Luca handled everything else. Loans, accounting, hiring. The less inspiring aspects of running a business.

The fact that not one, not two, but three firms passed on the buyout is a slap in the face.

"We're in a risk-averse market right now," Luca says. Though I don't even know if he comprehends what that means. He simply married an ambitious woman and did everything in his power to make her dreams come true—and he may have picked up an impressive phrase or two along the way. We both know I was always the brains in this operation.

"So what now?"

He stares at the wall behind me, his knuckles rapping on his thigh. "We fold."

This is the bottom dropping out. I thought it'd hit harder, but so far it feels like nothing—a dark void of numbness.

"What else?" I cross my arms and will him to look at me, but like a stubborn mule, the bastard refuses. "What else have you been keeping from me?"

He sniffs. "There's nothing more I can tell you that you don't already know."

"Come on. We *both* know that's a lie."

I turn and head to the hallway. I don't want to fight within earshot of my children. Oblivious or not, it's not the kind of precedent I want to set for this family.

"I'm done pretending," I say. "I'm done playing the role of your ignorant, dutiful wife. And I'm done biting my tongue when what I should be doing is asking you the *one* question that's been on my mind since the moment that woman showed up at our door."

He studies a vintage oil portrait on the wall behind me, lips pressing into a hard line like he's buying time.

"We promised we'd never talk about that," he finally says. And it's true. We've made a dozen ironclad agreements to one another since the beginning, but that was the biggest, most sacred one. Almost more sacred than our actual wedding vows.

"What choice have you left us?" I want to scream these words in his face until I'm bloodred. I want to push him against the wall, watch him stumble backward, and relish in the shocked look on his face as he's caught off guard. His sweet little wife, the mother of his children, the one woman he never should've underestimated.

His cheeks flush pink, though he's not embarrassed. Luca Coletto doesn't get embarrassed. He's frustrated, powerless, caught in a years-old lie by the *only* person who has ever stood by his side and loved him unconditionally.

"I'm going to give you one shot at this." I keep my voice low and my stare laser focused. "And if you lie to me, Luca . . . so help me . . ." Fist clenching midair, I ask the million-dollar question: *"Why is she still alive?"*

Elsie giggles from the next room, and I peek my head around the doorway to make sure Everett is safe.

One of us has to care.

"I'm wondering the same thing," he says, eyes tracking me. "I thought she was dead when I left."

"You didn't . . . I don't know . . . check her pulse?"

"I didn't want to touch her." He maintains an impressively stoic expression. "I shot her in the back, I watched her collapse, watched her bleed out. And I waited. I didn't want to move her or risk getting touch DNA or anything on or around her."

I roll my eyes. "Apparently you didn't wait long enough."

I've pegged him as many things over the years. Imbecile was the least of them. Until now.

Jaw clenched, I shake my head. "You've royally screwed us. You know that, right? And what were you thinking, bringing us out here? She's going to think we skipped town, and she's going to go straight to the police and turn you in."

"Trust me, she won't."

"And how do you know that?"

"Because I have something she wants." He tucks his chin. "She asked for a new identity, and I told her I'd handle it. She's not going to turn me in without getting what she wants."

Idiot.

"And what would she do with a stolen identity, Luca? Honestly." I throw my hands in the air and let them fall against my sides with a defeated, exaggerated clap.

He begins to say something, then stops.

"So much for being a team." I deliver my words with sharp precision, using a tone I've seldom used in this marriage.

"I've got a plan; you just have to trust me."

I run my fingers through my hair. "And does this plan have anything to do with my emptied bank account? And all those credit card withdrawals?"

"Yes, actually." He studies me with such intensity he doesn't blink. Perhaps he's trying to gauge my madness. Or maybe he's wrapping his head around a version of his wife he hasn't seen in years.

Years ago, I retired my ball-busting side in favor of a peaceful marriage, one built for the long haul. In retrospect, that appears to have been a mistake. Never give a horse too much rein lest he think *he's* the one leading the excursion.

"And you didn't think to *maybe* keep me in the loop before cleaning me out?" I could punch him—and I'm not a violent person. I've never hurt another human being in my life, but I'm willing to make an exception in his case. "I couldn't even buy *groceries*."

"She was extorting us," he says, "with that bullshit assistant manager position. A thousand bucks a day or she was going to turn me in. I had no choice."

"You were paying her *a thousand dollars a day*?" I clamp a hand over my nose and force a breath. No wonder he kept that from me—it probably would've sent me into an even earlier labor.

"I was giving her what she wanted so she'd leave us alone—and to buy us some time."

"Time to do what? Come up with another one of your brilliant ideas?"

I've never spoken to my husband with this tone of voice before—then again, I've never needed to. He's always been docile, agreeable . . . compliant. He knew how to give me what I wanted. And in return, I gave him what he wanted—a pretty little unopinionated housewife with a healthy sex drive and a promise to be loyal, faithful, and true come what may.

We were playing roles, he and I.

A well-oiled marital machine.

I'd always thought anyone else would be so lucky to have what we had—mutual respect, an understanding, a desperate want for the same things in life . . . financial security, love, a family.

I lean against the peeling floral wallpaper behind me, biting a defiant cuticle and taking a break from having to stare at a face that infuriates me more with every passing second.

A face *I* created, I might add.

He didn't look like this when we first met. He was my next-door neighbor—a greasy, unkempt diner busboy. A wallflower of a man with no friends, lacking a thread of charisma or social skills. But I saw something in him no one else did—untapped potential.

All the man needed was a haircut, a gym membership, a new wardrobe, and a vote of confidence. It was like watering a dying plant and shoving it in the sunlight. With a little time and a careful hand, I could bring this man to life. Make him a better version of himself . . . the version he was always meant to be.

Luca was perfect for what I needed. The only problem was, he was broke. Ramen noodle, rusted muffler broke.

I was picking him up from work one night when I spotted him awkwardly chatting it up with a mousy little thing outside the back door who clearly wanted nothing to do with him.

That's when Lydia Glass landed on my radar.

With nothing better to do, I dug into her past, nosed into her present, and gifted her with a future. The entire plan was my idea. The wooing. The whirlwind relationship. The quickie marriage in Vegas. Relocating to Bent Creek. The insurance policy. All of it.

The girl had no one. No friends, no family, no roommate. No life beyond waiting tables and bingeing Netflix shows in her shitty studio

195

apartment above some sex offender's garage. Everything about her screamed that she hated her life anyway. I could see it in those shit-brown eyes, the way she was waiting for someone to put her out of her misery.

If Luca was my moldable, pliable clay, Lydia was my low-hanging fruit. And together, they formed an illuminated path to the handcrafted, enviable life I deserved.

After their marriage and subsequent move to Bent Creek, I waited patiently for three months. While the two of them settled into "married life," I settled for secret rendezvous with Luca, ensuring he knew I'd be waiting for him in the wings when all this was over. And when the opportunity to take Lydia finally presented itself, I had to lie low for another year as he played the part of the grieving husband searching for his missing wife. There couldn't be another woman in the picture—at all. Armchair investigators and police alike would've been all over that.

"You know, no one told you to keep her alive for nine years . . ." I sigh. While I'll never admit it out loud, I blame myself for allowing it. Luca has demons. I've known that since several months into our relationship, when I stumbled across his collection of torture porn and the Polaroids of disfigured animals.

Most women would've run screaming in the other direction, but I'd already made progress with the man, and our plan was in motion. If I left him, he could've turned me in for plotting Lydia's kidnapping and murder. I had too much to lose by leaving and the entire world to gain by staying.

It was easier to move forward with my plan, to continue molding Luca into his ideal self. He could have his drowned-rat plaything if it meant I got the best parts of him. And if it hadn't been her, it would've been some other girl. Or girls. Plural. At least this way, we minimized his risk of getting caught.

Regardless, what's done is done. We can't change what he did or didn't do.

"We had a plan." I lift a hand to my head, forming the nozzle of a gun. We were three months along with Everett when I told him he needed to end it. It was time for him to bury his darkness and be a full-time family man. No more weekly visits to the cabin. No more pretending that side of him didn't exist—we needed to burn that part of him to the ground. "All you had to do was stick to it."

Everett cries in the next room, and my swollen breasts throb.

"Go get the groceries." I walk away.

I'll deal with him later.

CHAPTER

THIRTY-FOUR

LYDIA

The Coletto house is dark Tuesday evening when Jolie and I pull up. I went into the restaurant today to keep up with appearances—and to ensure no one called the bastard to let him know I didn't show up. Didn't want him to think I was up to anything. At the end of the dinner rush, I asked the chef to make Luca and Merritt's favorite meals, and then I caught a ride from Jolie on the way out.

"You think they're home?" I ask when she shifts into park.

She shrugs. "I don't know where else they'd be. They just had a baby . . . you want me to go with?"

"No, wait here. I'll be right back."

With bags of food in tow, I head to the front door and give it a light knock, then a second, slightly louder knock. There are no footsteps on the other side. No screaming baby or overzealous toddler. No humming TV or droning vacuum.

Heading around to the back of their house, I climb the stairs leading up to a set of sliding doors. Hands pressed against the glass; I stare into a dim and lifeless house. An empty sippy cup rests on the kitchen island, and the only light glowing is the one above the range. Heart ricocheting in my chest, I knock on this door.

"Merritt?" I call. "You home?"

Pressing my ear against the door, I listen—but even if there were something on the other side, the sound of the crashing ocean behind me would drown it out.

"Merritt." I pound on the glass, then move to the window beside it, trying to steal a better glimpse of what's inside.

A shadowy family room. Messy blankets piled on the sofa. A black TV screen. A remote control lying on the floor, as if someone dropped it but didn't have the need to pick it up.

Did they leave in a hurry?

And where the hell would they go with a newborn baby in tow?

The back deck spans the entire length of the Coletto house, and I move from window to window, cataloging every detail as if I'm inspecting a crime scene. The mess in the family room could be explained—but the scene in the master suite is concerning. Opened dresser drawers with clothes dripping down the sides. An unzipped toiletry bag on the foot of the bed. The light in the closet, left on and forgotten.

I peel my hands from the glass, leaving two perfect handprints that evaporate into thin air.

If something has happened to Merritt or the kids, the police will find my handprints all over these windows . . . and the motive will practically write itself.

She's crazy . . .

She wanted revenge . . .

She wanted it all . . .

Even if Luca goes down in the end, he'll make damned sure to take me with him.

Sucking in salty, shallow breaths, I carry the cold food back to Jolie's idling car.

"They aren't home." I buckle in and stare at the two perfect circles her headlights make on their wooden garage doors.

"That's weird." Jolie shifts into reverse, and when we're on the main road, she fusses with the music before settling on some Calexico. She doesn't think twice about any of it.

But I do.

All I can think about are those insurance policies on Merritt and Elsie.

If the man would kill me for two mil and a fresh start, who's to say he wouldn't do it to his new family? He has no conscience. No remorse. It'd be another Tuesday in his world.

Jolie drops me off in front of The Blessed Alchemist fifteen minutes later. Sprinting inside, I find Delphine at the kitchen table picking at a frozen dinner.

"Can you give me a ride to the police station?" I ask, breathless from climbing the stairs two at a time. "I'll explain on the way there."

Without saying a word, she pushes her chair out and grabs her car keys.

This—whatever it is, whatever it isn't, whatever it's going to be—is bigger than me.

I realize now . . . I can't do this alone.

CHAPTER THIRTY-FIVE

MERRITT

I stare at my useless credit cards Tuesday evening. I have half a mind to cut them up with kitchen scissors, to destroy them the way Lydia's destroying my family. The nerve of that woman to extort us like that.

A thousand dollars a day?

Who does she think she is?

And after I was so kind to her with the lunches and shopping, opening up to her as if she were a trusted friend.

I toss the cards back into my purse, not bothering to slide them into their wallet slots. And I head to the sink to rinse a head of cauliflower for the soup I'm making for dinner. I barely have the energy to feed my baby, but if I don't eat, neither will he.

With a razor-sharp butcher knife in hand, I chop the rinsed head into tiny pieces and dump them into a stock pot on this godforsaken electric range. I pour in a carton of bone stock and measure out a handful of spices before heading to the fridge for the butter, cream, and parmesan.

My first mistake was underestimating that woman. I was so convinced I could stay one step ahead of her by feigning ignorance, by rolling over like a submissive puppy and showing my vulnerable side. She could hate Luca all she wanted, but no one in their right mind would hurt a kind, generous, helpless pregnant mother.

Guess she wanted to get us where it counted—our pockets.

The conniving bitch played me like a fiddle . . . no easy feat.

I should have dealt with her myself when I had the chance. I easily could have invited her to lunch, slipped a little something into her drink—eye drops maybe—waited for her to pass out on the way home, then taken her out to a remote section of the woods to dispose of her. A quick slit to the jugular would've done it. No need to complicate it. But every time I played the scene out in my head, it always ended with that psychic lady she lives with giving interviews on TV, pointing fingers at Luca. Those types will do whatever they can to hog the spotlight, and free publicity is priceless. Not to mention, it's always the husband.

We've been screwed since the moment she ambled into town.

She was always the one in control—we merely had the illusion of it.

I measure a cup of heavy cream and dump it into the pot.

Never saw the extortion coming. Never in a million years. And a thousand bucks a day? I *still* can't get over it. She's bold, this one. That must be like lottery money to her. She could buy hundreds of canvas shoes with that kind of money . . .

In the next room, Luca tends to our children. Our beautiful, perfect, beloved babies. Does he realize how lucky he is that I chose him in the first place? I easily could've moved to a bigger city, set my sights on some moneyed doctor or established businessman, and taken a golden elevator to the top. But that's what my mother did—and we all know how that turned out for her.

Hand-selecting Luca to be my husband—my life partner—felt like an insurance policy against that sort of thing.

He was opposite of my father in every way. Head to toe. Inside and out.

It was easier than I expected, shaping Luca into what I wanted. Enjoyable too. Then again, it was probably the artist in me. Crafting beauty out of nothing.

It started with the little things—bathing him in attention and compliments unlike any he'd ever experienced. Making him believe he was a perfect catch exactly how he was. Constant reminders of how sexy I found him despite having to close my eyes and pretend he was anyone else just to climax.

I made him feel like a man . . . a *real* man . . . and eventually he started to act like one.

It wasn't an overnight process; in fact, it was a painstaking, years-long endeavor. But good art always takes time. But by the time we said "I do" on a private beach in Waikiki, the man was a *masterpiece*.

I stir the soup with a wooden slotted spoon, set the pathetic metal burner to simmer, and secure the lid.

Luca *hates* cauliflower—he also hates soup for dinner. *It's an appetizer, not an entrée,* he says. Hardly filling. But he's well aware of his current standing in my book, so he's not going to complain. He'll lap it up with a smile on his face if he knows what's good for him.

And if he's got a shred of brains left after the conversation we had earlier, he'll stay out of my way until I decide what to do with him.

CHAPTER THIRTY-SIX

LYDIA

Detective Nolan Rhinehart sits across from me, a steady hand covering his mouth as he forces a breath through narrow nostrils. He's young for a detective, maybe a little older than me. Maybe that means he's good at his job, that they promoted him into this position based on his competence and not the number of years he's put in.

"I know there isn't a name for this kind of thing," I say. Missing people don't usually come back, not after this long. At least not enough for there to be a dedicated word in the dictionary for this sort of thing.

Returned?

Restored?

I was simply missing, and now I'm *un*missing.

"So maybe there isn't a protocol," I continue, filling the silence with sound.

His eyes narrow. Either he doesn't believe me, or he's processing everything I've shared. Both, maybe.

"But whatever you need me to do to prove my identity," I say. "Fingerprints. DNA. Name it. I'll do it."

"I was a recruit, just started at the law enforcement academy when Lydia went missing." He sits straight. "She—*you*—were all anyone could talk about in my Investigative Procedures class." He reaches for a pen, tapping it on the dirty table. "I even volunteered all my free time to help search. We combed those woods around the clock for weeks."

Fullness presses behind my eyes. If I was capable of crying, I would. I walked in here with my defenses up, prepared to go to war to prove my case if needed. Fully expecting to be laughed at, stared at, ridiculed.

"You believe me," I say.

"Couldn't forget that face if I tried." He taps his pen again, nodding to himself as he looks down, lost in thought. "I was there the day we found your backpack on the cliffs." His jade-green eyes lock on mine. "Always found it fascinating that they were able to declare you dead without a body. Doesn't always happen that easily."

Knowing that man, what he's capable of, I'm sure there was some bribery involved or some loophole exploited.

"When you're about to get a windfall and you know the right people," I say, "you can make things happen."

"I don't like to speculate without the facts," he says, his tone direct yet placid. "But we'll figure it out."

While I've only known Detective Rhinehart two hours, he strikes me as a patient man. Unfortunately, his patience underserves this situation. I need someone to move on this *now*.

"I don't know where they are right now, but his wife and kids are in danger." I nudge the stack of papers closer to him and flip to the policy declaration pages. "If he did this to me, he'll do it to them."

He draws in a slow breath, scanning the papers. "It's not unusual for someone to take a policy out on their family members—and it's certainly not against the law."

"But given this man's history with insurance policies . . ."

He grimaces. "There's an order to everything. If he'd been charged with this crime, we might have probable cause to—"

"So because he got away with it, you're not going to do anything?" I don't mean to interrupt, but come on.

"I'm more concerned with getting your case closed, Lydia," he says. "And while *I* know it's you, we've still got to go through the proper channels. Probably start with a DNA test . . ." He exhales, cheeks inflating as his voice trails into his own silent thoughts. Making a quick note on his legal pad, he continues, "And in the meantime, we'll have to piece together your story a bit more. Solidify it if we can. You say you've been off the grid the last ten years . . . could be tricky. Definitely going to take some time. We'll also need to bring in Mr. Coletto for—"

"There isn't going to be a Mr. Coletto to bring in if you don't find him." I rise. "I'm telling you, he took his wife and kids, and he's going to do something to them. I know it."

He studies me, leaning back in his chair. "Do you know where he might've gone?"

I shrug. "No idea."

"At any time, did Mr. Coletto state he was going to harm them?"

My jaw falls slack. "No offense, Detective, but did you not hear a word I said? This man is a sociopath and a murderer, and he's got five million dollars waiting for him if he does what I think he's about to do. What I *know* he's about to do . . ."

"Yeah." He chews the inside of his lip. "I heard it all. Problem is, I can't go to my sergeant and tell him we've got to put out a search party for some family all because some woman walked in off the streets with a hunch." Before I can protest, he lifts a palm. "No offense to you either. Not saying I don't believe you, but that's not how this works. Unless we have evidence or probable cause, some reason to think his wife and kids are in immediate danger, legally there's nothing we can do."

I collapse into the opposite chair and bury my face in my hands.

If I can't save Merritt and the kids from The Monster, I'll never forgive myself.

"Other issue is, there was a reward fund set up for you," he says. "Can't remember the exact amount, but it was meant to encourage people to come forward with information leading to your whereabouts. Obviously that never happened, but a few years back, we had some lady wander in claiming she was you. Looked nothing like you and refused to let us swab her, so it wasn't hard to turn her away. But on the off chance you're not Lydia . . ."

"No, I understand. You have to do your vetting. I get it."

"If you want to wait here, I'll go grab a DNA swab kit. We can at least collect that while you're here." Rhinehart heads for the door.

"What are you going to do if there's no DNA to compare it to?" I ask.

"Got any family you can call? Someone we can use as a positive identifier?"

I shake my head. My mom—who was an only child—is dead. Couldn't even begin to guess my father's name. Never met a single grandparent. Never had a cousin that I know of.

"None that I can think of," I say.

His head tilts. "Surely there's someone."

I shrug. "Nope."

"I'll dig into your file. You'd be surprised who comes out of the woodwork when someone goes missing."

"I won't hold my breath."

He gives a terse nod. "Wait here, okay? I'll be right back."

Detective Rhinehart returns two minutes later with a sterile kit and swabs my nose and mouth before sealing it in a baggie, which he labels with my name.

"I'm sure this feels a bit anticlimactic for you," he says. "After all you've been through, I mean. But this is step one. We'll send it off to the lab, get it in our database, go from there."

"How long will this take to process?"

His eyes apologize before his mouth gets a chance. "Could take weeks? I'll have my sergeant see if he can move it to the top of the pile as a personal favor."

"What do I do in the meantime?"

His brows rise. "In the meantime, don't go anywhere. Don't do anything. Stay away from Mr. Coletto. Rest assured I'll be keeping an eye on him."

"But what if he doesn't come back to Bent Creek?"

"You let me worry about that, okay?" Sliding a yellow pad and pen across his desk, he adds, "Write down your name and number here. I'll get ahold of you once I talk to my sergeant."

I rise and gather my things. Delphine's been waiting for me in the waiting room this entire time, probably propped up in a hard chair summoning every archangel she can think of.

I jot down the address to The Blessed Alchemist and grab my phone to get the phone number. With everything going on, I've yet to take the time to memorize it. But it's then, as I'm tapping through my settings, that I take a second look at Luca's last text message.

The coordinates. It's a location. A lure.

I think I know where I might find them . . .

CHAPTER
THIRTY-SEVEN

We finish our cauliflower soup, get the babies to bed, and retire to the quiet dark of the living room. Everett has taken a turn for the better since we've been here. Less fussing, more eating. No more of that purple-faced screaming. Growing more wide-eyed and responsive by the hour.

Luca hasn't said a word all evening, though I watched him pop a couple of Advil and chug a bottle of water earlier. In the past, I'd massage his neck whenever he had a headache.

He can massage his own neck now.

"You need to replace the furnace filter," I call over my shoulder when I spot Luca heading from the kitchen to the stairs. If I didn't know better, I'd think he was avoiding me. "The air quality in here leaves much to be desired. It can't be good for the baby."

"I know." He stays planted at the base of the stairs, one hand on the railing. He couldn't hide the resentment in his voice if he tried.

"And we should wash Elsie's bedding," I add. "It's dusty."

"Yep."

So this is what it's come to.

Our handcrafted partnership is grinding to a screeching, resentful halt—and by no fault of my own, I might add.

This is all *his* doing.

I'll never forget that first year after the insurance windfall, how we reinvented ourselves. New clothes. New cars. A new-ish construction house in the suburbs. We waited two years after Lydia's official "death" before eloping, and we exchanged vows in a Hawaiian ceremony with a couple of locals as our witnesses.

When we came back to Bent Creek, we bought a dilapidated old boathouse not far from the shore and turned it into our first restaurant brainchild—Coletto's by the Sea. At the time, it was arguably the nicest eatery the town had ever seen, and we propped our reputation on catering to the well-to-do with money to burn.

My father always said the only way to make money was to have money first. It was a strange circle of logic that proved to be true. The more money we'd dump into the restaurant, the more money it would make—like a slot machine rigged in our favor.

With each flourishing year, we'd open another restaurant, and another. And at the peak of our success, we were pulling in a healthy seven figures. Of course, half of that went to taxes and another chunk went back into the business, but we were doing well for ourselves. More than well. We had everything we wanted—except a family.

Then came Elsie.

And Everett.

But now we're back to square one: miserable, penniless, hopeless.

All the control I had over him . . . Poof. Gone.

He said he had a plan, but it doesn't matter. I didn't need to ask him to elaborate because I've always been the one in control. He was the head, but I was the neck that moved the head.

Regardless, what's done is done.

And I've made my decision.

Friday morning, I'm driving into town to get my staples removed and to get the all-clear from the local OB. Afterward, I'm stopping into the bank to open an account so I can get a line of credit to cash out. When I get back, I'm packing up the kids and leaving Luca.

It's over.

CHAPTER

THIRTY-EIGHT

LYDIA

I stop into the restaurant Wednesday morning to use the computer. The prep cooks blare nineties music and clang around in the kitchen—I doubt they even know I'm here.

Pulling up a search engine, I type in the coordinates from Luca's text. I'd have done it from Delphine's computer last night, but she took it to bed with her, falling asleep to some movie she streamed to calm herself down after the interesting night we'd had. After leaving the police station, we stopped at an all-night pancake place, where she loaded up on processed junk and ranted my ear off about the inherent incompetency of the modern police system.

I'd never seen her so frazzled.

I let her fume. But while I pretended to listen, I was coming up with a plan of my own.

As frustrated as I was after leaving the station, Detective Rhinehart was right. Unless I give him evidence that someone's in danger, there's nothing he can do. And until they can legally prove I'm Lydia Glass/Coletto, everything is in limbo.

One thing at a time . . .

I type the final number of the coordinate and press "Enter," tugging at the protective crystal necklace Delphine gave me. I've yet to take it off—not because I believe in that stuff, but because I know it makes her feel better, and I've already put her through enough worrying.

The top result is a former real estate listing for some house in Willow Branch, Oregon. I click on the heading and scroll through the photos that load. All forty-two of them. Upon first glance, it's nothing more than an old farmhouse. White paint. Red barn. Small pond. Green everything. Picturesque but nothing flashy. Certainly not the kind of thing I'd imagine Luca and Merritt acquiring. It doesn't quite fit their Maserati lifestyle . . .

At the bottom of the page is a sales history, claiming it was purchased three years ago for seven hundred fifty grand. Next to the total is a hyperlink connecting to the county assessor's page. I can't imagine any scenario in which I'd need to know the property taxes on this thing, but I click it anyway.

Scrolling down a khaki-colored page filled with little white squares of information—acreage shape, square footage, outbuildings . . . I stop when I get to the owner line.

Luca and Merritt S. Coletto

I shove the chair out from under me and pace the tiny confines of my office.

He sent me that location along with the words "for your fresh start." Then he got out of town without telling anyone here where he went—I've asked.

If he were an actual human being with a bleeding heart, I'd almost think he was giving me this property.

But since I know The Monster, I know better.

It's bait.

And I'll bite.

Only this time, I'll be prepared.

CHAPTER

THIRTY-NINE

Wind howls through the drafty farmhouse window as I feed Everett. I'm not sure the time—somewhere between two and three AM if I had to guess. Luca and Elsie are asleep. The house should be silent, only it isn't. It never is. This old thing creaks and moans day and night, never shutting up.

If I believed in ghosts and that sort of nonsense, maybe I'd wonder if this place is haunted by its previous owners—the Jamesons. Can't imagine building an entire life out here, raising your children and grandchildren in these picturesque rolling hills, only to have them cash in on your death the first chance they get.

Talk about a slap in the face.

My children will know what it means to appreciate where they came from.

Maybe the Jamesons were shitty parents who cared more about their farm than their family?

It's easy to idealize strangers, to view them through our own life lenses. Growing up, I would've sworn everyone had it better than me and that my parents were the only ones with an embarrassingly dysfunctional marriage. Now that I'm grown, I know better.

There's no such thing as a perfect marriage.

Though Luca and I came pretty damn close.

The floorboards settle from the hallway.

"Luca?" I call out, waiting.

Nothing.

Just the house adjusting, as per usual.

But then it happens again. Footsteps. Three of them. Then another. All spaced apart in random increments.

Placing the baby over my shoulder, I rise from the rocking chair and lumber to the door, peeking my head into the hall. But there's nothing. No one. Darkness and a few pictures on the walls.

With Everett in my arms, I make my way around the old house, stopping at Elsie's room to click off the sound machine. Luca always forgets to set the twenty-minute timer. Inhaling the scent of lived-in must and other people's memories, I linger over my daughter's bed for a moment and watch her sleep.

Someday soon *this* will be a memory.

After we leave, we're never coming back. I haven't decided where we're going yet. Maybe we'll make our way across the country and wind up in Manhattan at my sister's. It won't be ideal shacking up with her and her single-girl-in-the-big-city lifestyle, but until I'm able to get on my feet again—and I will—she's the best chance we have.

The windows rattle. They said a cold front was coming through tonight, but I don't remember hearing anything about a windstorm. Peeking beyond the lacy curtains, I can see the wall of leaning, stretching trees that line this side of the property. I suppose it makes sense then—this noise. We're not insulated out here. There's no cocoon protecting this house from the elements or outside threats.

With one hand, I adjust Elsie's covers in case it grows colder tonight. And then I carry the baby downstairs. I could easily put him to bed in his bassinet and climb in beside my husband and catch a few hours of sleep, but I'd rather hold him a little longer.

Everything's about to change.

I need to soak in these last little moments. Maybe do a little preemptive mourning.

It takes forever to get to the bottom of the stairs with Everett in my arms and my incision flinching with pain, but I make it. A minute later, I manage to get us settled in the microfiber La-Z-Boy, a throw blanket keeping us warm. Milk-drunk, my son falls asleep on my chest, his little chest swelling and emptying with each breath.

My lids grow heavy as I press my toes against the floorboards, rocking us both to sleep.

If everything goes to hell in a handbasket, at least I have my babies. There's nothing in this world more priceless than a child's love for their mother. Nothing in this world that can take it away. That's the thing about children, they love without reason, without fear, and without condition.

It never mattered that my mother sent me away year after year, that she could never sit through a family gathering without having downed a gin and tonic and a benzo. Or that she forgot my birthday more times than I could count over the years. I still loved her. And I still miss her every day.

I rub Everett's back, press my cheek against his silky hair, and breathe in his powdery scent.

I don't need money, a luxury car, an enviable house, or a useless husband to validate my place in this world.

Everything I've done—and everything I'll ever do—is for my children.

Nothing else matters.

No *one* else matters.

I'm half-asleep when an upstairs door thumps shut. I'm certain I'm dreaming at first, that I must have jolted myself awake, until my husband's muffled voice fills the quiet air. He's been known to sleep-walk, and he's had more conversations in his sleep over the years than I can count. There's no way he'd make this much noise in the middle of the night on purpose. The man's an idiot, but he's not that stupid.

Settling back into the recliner, I stroke Everett's tender, newborn head and get comfortable again.

Until I hear a second voice.

A *female* voice.

CHAPTER FORTY

LYDIA

"What the—" The whites of Luca's eyes illuminate the dark.

I switch on the lamp beside Luca's bed the second I'm done securing him to the metal headboard. A pile of extra zip ties sits on the nightstand, along with a roll of duct tape and a butcher knife I took from Delphine's kitchen on my way out. I was expecting Merritt to be in here with him, but when I got inside she was in a spare bedroom upstairs, feeding the baby. I managed to sneak by unseen, and then I crept into their room . . . waited . . . swallowing quiet breaths and taking slow, quiet steps so I wouldn't wake the bastard.

He was always a heavy sleeper—but on the off chance he woke up in the middle of this, I'd have been screwed. Two against one is never ideal, especially when one of the two has been brainwashed into rooting for the wrong team.

Luca yanks on the ties, the ones I've tightened so close to his flesh he'll probably have marks for days. I hop off the bed and move for the door, twisting the old-fashioned lock. Who knows if it'll hold by the time Merritt figures out something's going on up here, but it'll at least buy time.

I don't want to hurt that poor woman, and I certainly don't want to traumatize her, but she needs to hear me out. She needs to know who her husband is, what he's capable of, and what he's going to do to her and her children. If restraint is the only way to get her to listen, so be it.

"Lydia." He yell-whispers my name, spittle flying from his mouth. "The hell are you thinking?"

He doesn't plead for me to cut him loose. He doesn't try to reason with me with some psychobabble bullshit.

"What am I thinking?" I grab the knife, climb on their bed, and straddle him at the hips. "I'm thinking I'm the one who should do the talking here . . ."

I didn't secure his ankles—he was starting to stir, and his wrists were the priority.

He bucks beneath me, his legs kicking, trapped under a mountain of blankets and a heavy quilt.

If only there were time to appreciate the poetic justice of this moment—restraining the very hands that once restrained me.

"Don't." I press the tip of the knife against his neck, pointing it into the pulsating spot several inches below his jaw.

"Lydia, listen to me." His voice is barely above a whisper, but his eyes hold no fear. Not sure what I expected, though. I've known from the start that this man's incapable of feeling or showing genuine emotion. He may not be pissing his pants, but he knows he's at my mercy, and that's satisfying just the same. "If you kill me, that means no more cash. And that identity you wanted, I have it. The papers are in my suitcase. If you—"

"I don't want someone else's identity. I want mine." I press the blade flush against his hot skin. A superhuman rush of adrenaline floods my veins. I've never felt so powerful, so in control. This must have been what he felt all those times . . .

"Then why'd you come out here?" His dark brows gather below his worry-lined forehead. "Why didn't you just go to the police?"

Ha. If he only knew . . .

I don't answer him because a little wondering won't kill him—though I wish it could.

"I know all about your life insurance scheme." I nod toward the dresser, where I've placed the envelope containing the declaration pages. My original plan was to secure both Colettos with the ties, silence them with duct tape so I'd have their ears, and once I had Merritt calmed down, I was going to present my proof. Even if she didn't want to hear it, she wouldn't be able to argue with hard evidence. "You left in a hurry the other day, forgot to lock your office. It's amazing what a person can find if they look hard enough."

"You have no idea what you're talking about."

I ignore his feeble attempt at gaslighting. It doesn't work on me anymore. Not only is he an inhuman monster, he's a liar and a con. Nothing that leaves his mouth is to be trusted.

"You shouldn't have done this." He emphasizes every syllable, his eyes widening in a silent urge to read between the lines. Another pathetic attempt to manipulate me. "I know you think you're doing the right thing here, but trust me—you don't know the half of what you think you know."

I fight an incredulous chuckle. "Oh, yeah? Is that so? Please. Enlighten me."

Hours ago, I was sitting on the edge of my bed in Delphine's spare room, going through my plans for the evening for the millionth time. After she went to bed, I waited until I heard her faint snores, and then I sneaked out to the kitchen, plucked her phone off the charger, and ordered a ride to the farmhouse for $112—which I'll pay back with interest. For an extra twenty bucks, I got the driver to stop at a local twenty-four-hour Wal-Mart so I could grab a few things. And two hours later, we were pulling into the long gravel drive leading up to the chocolate-box farmhouse that matched the real estate listing photos.

"Luca?" Merritt's voice pushes through the wooden door, and the handle jiggles. "Luca, why's the door locked? Let me in . . ."

She raps on the door, loud enough to be heard but low enough that it wouldn't wake a sleeping child in the next room.

Our eyes lock. His lips press thin and his nostrils flare, but when he tries to respond, I flatten my palm over his mouth.

I was surprised to find their back door unlocked when I arrived. I mean, technically it was locked. The bolt had been shifted into the proper position. But a few hardy pushes were enough to jimmy it open. That's the thing with these old houses . . . they can't always be trusted. Something is always in disrepair, and you never realize it until the moment you actually need it.

"Luca," she says, louder this time. "Open the door."

He makes a face beneath my hand, a silent urge for me to do something. But the door stops jiggling and the floor creaks in the hall, as if she's walking away.

I lift my hand from his thin mouth.

"She's going to get a key," he whispers.

Shrugging, I say, "Then I guess we'll have some explaining to do in a minute, won't we?"

Maybe I shouldn't, but I find this entire thing amusing . . . even more amusing than the expression on his face when he walked into his house last month and saw me sitting at his kitchen table.

It was a precious little moment—one for the books.

But this is *priceless*.

"So what's your plan?" he asks.

"Wouldn't you like to know . . ."

"You've already destroyed my marriage. I've given you everything you need to get back on your feet. What are you going to gain from this?" He tugs at his restraints.

I remove the knife tip from his throat and climb off the bed to stretch.

"I want justice. And I want you to come clean to your wife about what you did," I say, adding, "and what you *are*."

"You want to know what I am?" He spits his words at me. "I knew you weren't dead when I left you there. I never wanted to kill you. You're only alive because I saved you."

"You're pathetic." And delusional if he thinks I'm believing a word out of his ugly mouth.

"You don't have to believe me, but it's true. I might be a lot of things, Lydia. I'm fucked up and I know it. But I'm not a murderer."

"You left me to die . . . I don't see how that redeems you."

I'd been captive for several years the night he choked on a handful of Marcona almonds. With a red face and blue lips, he gasped for air, mouthing directives for me to help him while I backed myself into the corner, praying for him to die.

In an unfortunate turn of events, he was able to clear the blockage himself.

But that moment has haunted me for years, that teasing proximity to freedom.

Would I have been a murderer if I'd left him to die?

"I shot you in the shoulder," he says, "with a nine millimeter. I knew it'd pass through. Most people can survive that."

"You couldn't have known that." I roll my eyes—mostly at myself for hearing him out. "You left me in the middle of nowhere, bleeding out . . ."

It wasn't the first time he made me bleed. I'd existed a mere three weeks with his monstrous alter ego when he appeared late one evening, knife, bucket, and gauze in tow. With dead eyes, he sliced the flesh of my stomach as I writhed against my restraints, filling the small container with my blood. I passed out after that. When it was over, I was bandaged, my muscles aching where he'd slashed through them. And when I slid a hand across my pulsing scalp, my fingertips grazed torn patches.

I know now that he used my blood and hair to stage a crime scene—something to make the police have reason to suspect I'd been killed and disposed of. A local medical examiner was quoted as saying, "It's highly unlikely a person could survive that kind of blood loss." That douche was instrumental in getting the judge to approve my death certificate.

Idiots.

All of them.

"You weren't going to die," he says. "I just didn't think you were stupid enough to come back."

The door busts open, slamming on the other side. Merritt's shadowy figure fills the narrow doorway, a skeleton key pinched between her fingers.

I expect him to solicit her help—or for her to react. But for an endless handful of seconds, the three of us are frozen in a silent standoff.

"Merritt," I say, breaking that silence. "I'm going to need you to stay calm."

Her watchful gaze passes between us.

"There's something you need to know about your husband." I nod toward the dresser. "Those papers over there—those are life insurance declaration pages. Luca has five million on you and your daughter."

The skeleton key lands on the floor with a metallic clunk before she strides across the room and gathers the papers in her hand. Squinting in the dim light, she studies the words, pages through the documents, and checks the backs.

Her clear, crystalline eyes turn a bone-chilling shade of blue from across the room as they narrow in on her husband.

Safe to say she didn't know about these . . .

"You *disgust* me." She spits her words at her husband, still residing on the opposite side of the room. "You're a sorry, pathetic excuse for a man."

Gone is the docile wife and mother I've come to know in recent weeks, and in her place is a woman scorned.

Standing back, I contemplate my next move. I thought it'd take more convincing. I thought I was going to have to argue my case a little harder than this . . .

"A million dollars on our *daughter*?" She waves the papers in the air, wrinkling them in her tightened fist. "What were you going to do, Luca?" Merritt drags a hand through her messy hair. "Did you put one on the baby, too?"

He doesn't say a word. In fact, he hasn't said a word since the door swung open and his wife joined the party.

"I wouldn't put anything past him," I say. "He's the one who took me. He held me captive for years. Staged my abduction so he could cash in on a two-million-dollar life insurance policy. And he tortured and raped me, week after week. He's the one who tried to kill me, who left me for dead. If he could do it to me, he could do it to you and your children, too. He's *sick*, Merritt. The worst kind."

"She knows." Luca's voice is low, defeated almost. And it takes a second for me to realize he's not speaking to Merritt. "She knows everything."

He's talking to *me*.

"The whole thing was her idea." Luca's lips tighten. "Tell her, Mer. Tell her you picked her yourself. Tell her you planned *every last detail*."

"You're a goddamned liar." My middle turns rock-hard, and the air around me thickens. I point my knife at his face, which suddenly feels no different than pointing a scrawny tree branch at someone wielding a gun. If this is true, it's two against one, and the odds are absolutely not in my favor.

With trembling hands, Merritt places the papers on the dresser, and then she turns to me, eyes glossy. "Don't listen to him, Lydia. He's lying. It's what he does. It's what he's good at. I've been uncovering them left and right these last few weeks . . ."

Luca yanks the restraints again, his legs flailing until the quilt and covers slide off the side of the bed and fall into a heap on the floor.

"*You're sick, Luca.*" Merritt points at him, her words terse. "We're leaving." Turning back to me, she places a hand over her lower stomach. "I hate to ask, Lydia, but can you help me get the kids in the car?"

He tugs harder this time, and his fingertips are pink-white from the lack of blood flow. "Don't listen to her, Lydia. Don't believe any of it."

A thick tear slides down Merritt's bare cheek, and she tucks her chin low as she heads for the door.

"You can't leave me like this." Luca writhes, digging his heels into the lumpy mattress. But all my years of knowing this bastard won't let me feel sorry for him. I follow Merritt. Whatever happens to Luca is no longer my responsibility. I'll get her out of here, hitch a ride to town, and go straight to the police. They can deal with him.

I'm officially done.

He carries on, yelling louder, screaming for someone to untie him.

"My keys are on the counter." She takes slow, careful steps down the hallway, stopping outside one of the bedroom doors. "If you could start the car for me . . ."

"Of course." I trot down the steps, find the BMW fob on the counter, and head outside. The headlights of her SUV blink when I get closer, and the door locks click. Once inside the driver's seat, I glance around the cockpit-esque dash and to the side of the steering wheel . . . until I realize I have no idea how to start this thing.

Abandoning the keys in the cup holder, I jog inside and follow the light upstairs, where I find Merritt, wrapping her sleeping daughter in a small blanket.

"Can you carry her to the car for me?" she asks, wincing as if she's both exhausted and in pain, though it's impossible to know if it's emotional or physical. "And buckle her in?"

Her daughter starts to wake, her sleep-heavy eyes scanning between us.

"It's okay, sweetheart." She rubs Elsie's back. "Mommy's friend is going to put you in your car seat. I'm getting your brother, and I'll be right there."

I take the toddler, who is heavier in my arms than I imagined, and I carry her down the rickety wooden stairs and out the front door. It's a strange thing, holding my abuser's child in my arms and carrying her to safety. Not something I ever imagined I'd be doing in my lifetime. But a minute later, she's buckled in and I'm on my way back for the other one.

Luca yells from his room. Louder. Harder. More desperate.

The baby whimpers in Merritt's arms.

She leans down, lips pressed against his cheek. *"Sh, sh, sh, sh . . ."*

Everything's happening in a vacuum—all at once and too fast to track.

"His car seat's in there." With a strangely calm air about her, Merritt nods toward the room at the end of the hall. Within seconds I retrieve a gray infant carrier, returning to place it by her feet. Carefully, she crouches down and straps the baby in before tucking a white muslin blanket around the lower half of his tiny body. He stirs, hands above his head and face in a pre-cry wince, but she silences him with a soft green pacifier. "I hate to ask you for another favor . . ."

"No, it's fine." It's the least I can do after the devastating news she's received—and less than a week after giving birth.

"The whole thing just . . . clicks into the base . . ." She motions with her hands, feigning the movements. "When you sit it on . . ."

"I'll figure it out." With a tight grip on the car seat, I head to the car. It takes a few tries, but eventually the seat clicks into the base. I double-check to make sure it's secure, and then I run back in. It's chilly out—and the car isn't running.

I find her in Elsie's room, tossing haphazardly folded clothes from the small chest of drawers into a slouchy duffel bag.

"I didn't know how to start the car," I tell her. Though her back is to the doorway, she doesn't startle. She simply continues to pack.

"Put your foot on the brake and then press the button by the shifter." She tugs the zipper closed and brings me the bag. "I've got to grab the diaper bag and my suitcase, and then I'm getting out of here."

Her voice is an unexpected shade of calm, and her eyes no longer hold the tears they brimmed with when she walked away from her conniving husband mere minutes ago. I learned long ago that people handle stress and trauma in all kinds of ways. Some of us fall apart at the seams. Others of us slip into action mode and reserve the emotions for later.

"You okay?" I ask. We're not exactly friends, but after everything we've been through, I think it's safe for me to ask.

She studies me in the dark, unblinking. "I will be."

The Merritt I first met was a portrait of insecurity and a fountain of anxiety. The Merritt standing before me is robotic and cold. But she's been through the unthinkable. Now's not the time to judge.

"I just want to focus on getting my kids away from . . . *him*." She slips past me and heads to the hall, stopping in the doorway to brace her hand against the frame. "It isn't safe here—for any of us."

Believe me, I know.

"I'm going to the police after this," I say. "I'm turning him in for everything. I could use your help."

Her lower lip trembles, and she hesitates. "Of course."

It's not ideal, what with the babies and all, but the two of us together would be a doubleheader of credibility.

It must be awful, losing the father of your children like this. Knowing he isn't dead, but he'll never be the man you fell in love with. And what will she tell their children? It's a fate worse than death, and I hate that this happened to them.

"Would you mind starting the car while I grab my suitcase?" She points to the open door, where Luca's screams still echo off the wallpapered walls.

Merritt disappears into the bedroom before I think to ask her to retrieve the papers (and Delphine's butcher knife), and I wait at the top of the stairs. I'll have to grab those before we leave.

Voices trail from the end of the hall. Some kind of heated exchange lightly muffled by these old walls. I pick out a handful of phrases: Luca pleading with her to cut the zip ties and Merritt calling him every name

227

under the sun but with a dignified condescension in her voice. A second later, the sound of luggage wheels against hardwood is followed by the slamming of a door. But before I can turn around to grab her suitcase, I'm hit with blinding, white-hot pain in the back of my head.

It takes me a moment to realize what happened, and while I'm now on the floor, I don't remember the fall. Reaching toward the pulsating throb in the back of my head, my fingertips turn wet with what I can only assume is blood. With blurred, starry vision that fades in and out with each heartbeat, I concentrate on the dark figure hovering over me.

"Merritt?"

I don't understand . . .

My thoughts crisscross in every direction as I try to wrap my mind around this, but the pain screams too loudly for me to make logical sense out of any of this.

"What happened to staying *as good as dead*?" Merritt repeats a phrase only Luca could have known, hands gripped tight around what appears to be a marble bookend.

No . . .

"This is what you get for coming back," she says, "for ruining *everything*."

Luca wasn't lying.

Merritt knew . . . she knew everything.

With the bookend clenched tight and a wicked leer painted on her face, Merritt strikes me once more.

Everything turns to black.

CHAPTER

FORTY-ONE

MERRITT

Lydia crumples into a motionless heap at my feet, her hair blanketing her shoulders and covering her boring, punchable face.

"Merritt!" My husband—*soon-to-be late ex-husband*—screams at me from down the hall. I'll cherish the day I never have to hear that voice again. "What are you doing? What was that?"

Oh—so now *he* gets to be the good one?

He gets to grow a conscience?

I shove my suitcase down the steps so I don't have to lug it myself. It rolls, slides, and topples before skidding across the foyer and stopping on its side near the front door. I could've waited for Lydia to lug it to the car for me, but when I came out of the bedroom and saw her standing at the top of the stairs, her back to me, the opportunity presented itself with perfection.

Without giving it a second thought, I swiped a marble bookend off the hall table and launched it at the back of her egg-shaped head with every jot of force I could muster.

Two strikes in total.

That's all it took.

I guess the old adage is true—if you want something done right, you've got to do it yourself.

My hands throb as I bend to examine her. Shoving her stringy hair aside, I place my palm in front of her nose. A veil of hot breath covers my skin.

She's not dead.

Not yet.

My incision throbs, but only for a second, and then I feel nothing. Forcing myself back up, I return to the bedroom. Now that Lydia's unconscious, I can say what I really want to say to this pathetic bastard.

Grabbing the policies off the dresser, I wave them in his face. "Five million, eh? That's all I'm worth to you?"

I don't know if I should be more insulted by the lowball price tag on my head or the fact that he thought he could pull this off behind my back—both are equally offensive in my book.

"Of course not." He doesn't blink, and his eyes hold zero fear. "That's the amount Brian recommended."

"Ah, yes. The guy who sells us our home and auto insurance. Let's blame everything on him. That'll make this go away, won't it?" I reach for the butcher knife, palming the cheap stainless steel handle. "So Brian, I take it, is the one who told you to take out a million-dollar policy on our two-year-old?"

"Tragic things happen all the time. It was a precaution."

"Did you take a policy out on yourself while you were . . . *indemnifying* our family?"

"Of course," he says. "We're *all* covered. You're blowing this out of proportion. It's smart financial planning. You're letting that stupid bitch fill your head with lies."

I tilt my head, frowning. She's not as dumb as one might think if she pieced together our entire plan after being back in our lives for less than a month . . .

"How'd she know where we were? You told me you wanted to bring us here to get *away* from her. What were you planning?" I examine the shiny blade of the knife in the dull lamplight. It's rust spotted, overused, but sharp *enough*.

"I've been wondering the same thing." He speaks through gritted teeth as if that might make any of this more convincing—and then he makes a grave mistake. For a fraction of a second, his soulless gaze snaps to his phone on the nightstand.

"Luca . . ." I feign a dramatic gasp. "Please tell me you didn't do what I think you did . . ."

He thrashes, tugging against the zip ties, and then the asshole has the audacity to try to kick me when I snatch his phone.

I tap in his code—our meaningless wedding anniversary—and pull up his messages, weeding through them until I find the last one he sent to Lydia: GPS coordinates along with the words "for your fresh start."

"You told her to come here?" I slam the phone down so hard the screen cracks in the corner. "Why? Why the hell would you do that?"

"I was going to finish the job." He tries to sit up, but he can't. I imagine he's extremely uncomfortable in this position and his back is probably screaming in pain, but his comfort is the least of my concerns. "I was going to get her out here, finish her off, and bury her under the barn or burn her . . . I don't know . . . The nearest neighbor is ten miles from here. No one would hear a thing, no one would *see* a thing. And as long as we keep the property in our name, no one will ever find her."

"Oh. My. God." I suck in a breath. "Is *that* what you were going to do with us?"

"No." His brows meet and his white tee rides up, exposing his softening gut. When did he stop taking care of himself? When he realized he no longer needed to impress me because I'd soon be dead?

"You were going to kill us all, weren't you?" I walk to the other side of the bed, pacing next to the window. "You were going to kill off all your problems—literally—and walk away a free and wealthy man."

I perch on the foot of the bed, mentally playing out this sick fantasy of his, imagining him driving down to the police station in a few days to report his wife had murder-suicided herself and the kids. He'd tell them I'd been hallucinating. He'd spin it like I was suffering postpartum psychosis and everything happened so quickly he didn't have time to get me the help I needed.

That poor widowed man, everyone would say. And then they'd focus on the dead babies. Because that's what people always think about in those situations. It tugs at their heartstrings as they imagine what it must have been like for the kids, to die at the hand of their own mother. And then they find it in their heart to have compassion for me because motherhood is hard. Especially new motherhood.

And Luca—he'd play the role of the mourning husband, a man twice struck by unthinkable tragedies. But as soon as that five mil hit landed in his hands, he'd be gone.

"Maybe you're not as stupid as I thought you were." I study him for the last time. And then I think of Lydia. He was supposed to kill her that first week. Make it quick. Instead he dragged it out for *years* as I turned a blind eye, my gift to him. And he screwed her—while he was screwing me, while he was planning a future with me, while he was *loving* me. While I played the role of his perfect wife, she filled his cup. She was always his satisfaction. "The joke's been on me this whole time, hasn't it?"

He stops squirming, his attention landing on the knife in my white-knuckled hand.

"Don't do this . . . think of the kids." He swallows, but all I can look at is the pulsing vein in his neck.

"The kids are *all* I think about." I inch closer. "Wish you could say the same."

"Where are they?"

I find it impossible to believe he cares about their whereabouts. He's trying to distract me, that's all.

"They're safe," I say. Though the car isn't running, I made sure they were wrapped in blankets before I sent Lydia down with them. They might be cold, but they're not freezing. And I'll be with them soon enough. "Not that you care. I mean, you *were* going to murder them . . ."

"That's not true. I swear on my *life*."

"I honestly thought you loved me." I roll my eyes at myself. "God, what an idiot I was. The player got played. Serves me right, I guess."

"I *do* love you." He writhes. "I love you more than anything. You *and* the kids. You're my world . . . the only thing that matters to me."

"Please." I yawn. "Save your tired greeting-card sentiments. Nothing you say is going to change any of this. It's too late to rewrite your future. And honestly, the one I wrote for you the first time around was pretty damn amazing. I'm sorry you couldn't see that."

This is his fault: the struggling businesses no one will buy, the mess we're in now, the fatherless childhood our children are about to know.

He opens his mouth to refute, but I'm tired. I can't subject myself to another miserable second of his voice, and my babies are getting cold.

Without warning, I plunge the butcher knife into the tender bend of his neck, and I climb off the bed before any of the gushing blood spills onto my nightgown.

Luca tries to speak, but his voice is gurgled.

Murder weapon in hand, I filch the extra zip ties off the nightstand—displeased at the thought of Lydia tying me up in this scenario. I close the door behind me, leaving my husband to choke to death on his own blood.

Honestly, he did this to himself.

All he had to do was listen to me, respect me, trust that I had *all* our best interests at heart. Lydia was a nuisance, yes, but I would've made it all go away had he kept me in the goddamned loop and not treated me like the Golden Globe–worthy character I played.

The elfin woman hasn't moved an inch, still lying in a heap by the stairs. I check her breath again. Unfortunately still alive. Exhaling, I yank the god-awful necklace from around her neck and wrap it twice around my wrist like a makeshift bracelet.

A last-minute souvenir, something I can pull out of a drawer someday when life is excruciatingly hard and I need a reminder of the mountain I scaled to get there.

Gripping the handrail, I make my way downstairs—to the fireplace. I strike a match from the box on the mantel and toss it into the log pile in the firebox, along with the remaining zip ties and the blood-soaked butcher knife. Tiny flames curl around a small piece of firewood, slowly wrapping the length before spreading to the one above.

I light four more matches, throw them all in, and grab the fire stoker. A minute later, I've arranged enough of the kindling outside the firebox to help it spread beyond the brick surround before it crawls toward a nearby children's book, then to a blanket and a throw pillow next to the sofa.

While I'd love to stay and watch the entire place burn to the ground, I must be on my way.

Grabbing my purse from the kitchen table, I exit from the farmhouse for the final time, slide into my cold car, and start the engine. I press the seat and steering wheel warmers and let it idle for a bit, checking on my sleeping babies, who are none the wiser.

Someday, when they're old enough to understand, I'll tell them all about their father's deranged first wife, how she faked her disappearance and came back with a vengeance, jealous of his idyllic new life. I'll tell them how she sneaked into our beautiful farmhouse when we were asleep, tied their father up, and stabbed him in the jugular. With tears in my eyes, I'll describe in meticulous, heartfelt detail how the three of us narrowly escaped death after Lydia lit a fire in our living room and tried to barricade us inside until I mustered the strength to fight back and get us to safety.

I give the fire a little more time to spread before shifting into reverse and heading to town. According to my GPS, we're twenty minutes from the police station. By the time I get there, I'll have my story together.

I dump my phone in a dumpster outside a gas station on the edge of town; that way I can say I had no means to call 911. She took my phone, I'll tell them. It perished in the fire . . . along with my poor husband. And when they get there and find her dead of smoke inhalation, they'll rule it a murder-suicide. No questions asked.

Thirty days from now, I'll submit my claim against the life insurance policy I took out on my husband years ago—the one I purchased *just in case*.

A precaution of my own.

Because I am—by all accounts—a reasonable woman.

CHAPTER
FORTY-TWO

LYDIA

I wake with a gasping start, my lungs burning. Everything around me is dark, and the smoky scent of fire and ash fills my nostrils. Feeling the ground around me, I slick my hand against the top step in an attempt to get my bearings, but when I push myself up, my head throbs and everything around me turns on its side.

If I crawl down the stairs, I could hurt myself.

But if I stay here, I'll die.

Consciousness eludes me, my surroundings morphing from gray smog to blackness and back. Between flashes of reality, the furious red-orange glow of flames licks the ceiling above, coming closer, burning hotter, taking no prisoners.

A flame spark drips from the ceiling, landing on the top of my hand, sending a blinding-hot shock of pain across my flesh that almost renders me unconscious again. I jerk my hand away from the hot spot, pressing it against my chest and breathing through the throbbing sting—only every breath suffocates me further, drowning me in smoke.

Stretching my feet, I feel for the top step, and with weak, shaking arms, I slide myself to the first tread. Then another. And another. Gasping for air that never feels like enough, I lose count of the stairs.

Everything around me grows dim, and I'm certain this is it. I'm going to die here, in this house in the middle of nowhere, going down in flames with the devil himself.

Until the woman in white appears—her flowing dress a beacon of hope. Hooking her arms beneath mine, she drags me down the rest of the stairs, across the foyer, and over the threshold of the front door, and she doesn't stop until we reach a blanket of cool, wintry earth beneath a sky full of stars.

"You're safe now, angel," she says. "Help is on the way."

My eyes sting, and my vision is blurred. Rolling to my side, I cough and gasp and clutch the dormant grass beneath my body like the lifeline it is—like the lifeline it was the first time I almost died.

Crouching beside me is the woman in the white dress, a green-black stone dangling from her neck as she pats my back the way a mother would comfort her child.

I don't know how; I don't know why.

Fire roars and crackles from the house as it folds in on itself, one piece of timber at a time. Sirens wail in the distance until they grow so close my ears ache. Everything fades to gray, though for how long, I can't be certain. When I come to, an oxygen mask covers my face and two people load me onto a stretcher.

I've never believed in guardian angels before.

I still don't.

Who needs one of those when I have Delphine?

She climbs into the back of the ambulance. Sliding her hand in mine, she reserves the lecture I know is brewing in that merciful, crinkled gaze of hers. And instead she gives me nothing but her support, her calming presence, and an unspoken reminder that we don't always have to do things alone.

EPILOGUE

LYDIA

Two Weeks Later

"Feel like a walk?" Delphine raps on my bedroom door on this lazy Sunday afternoon. Part of my recuperation requires an abundance of fresh air to keep my body oxygenated and my lungs functioning. The doctors say I'll make a full recovery. The smoke inhalation was minor, and they promise that someday soon my lungs won't burn every time I take a breath.

I flip the covers off my legs. "Yeah."

She doesn't offer to help me out of bed. I'm not helpless. Not anymore. The first couple of days home, I let her dote on me, but it was mostly for her benefit. Delphine is a caretaker. She needs to be needed. And because she literally saved my life, I wanted to at least give her that.

She waits for me by the door, placing my slip-on shoes side by side because she can't help herself. And then she grabs two waters from the fridge. A minute later, we're ambling down the semicrowded sidewalks of Bent Creek, passing families on spring break and locals out for a Sunday stroll.

"Detective Rhinehart called this morning," I say.

"Yeah? Any updates?"

"They're still waiting to hear back from the lab, but he wanted to tell me about the reward money . . . there's almost seventy grand in there, and he says it's all mine once they can confirm everything."

"That's wonderful, angel."

I've been thinking lately about timing—or divine intervention, as Delphine likes to call it. The night I ordered a ride using Delphine's phone, she woke in the middle of the night after a fiery nightmare, parched, something that rarely happens to her. Half-asleep, she shuffled out to the kitchen to grab a drink . . . which was when she spotted the notification on her phone from the rideshare app. Within minutes, she pieced it all together, raced to her car, and programmed the coordinates into her navigation app.

She was an hour behind me.

But looking back, even a minute could've been the difference between life and death.

She was barreling down the highway, about to turn on their road when she spotted the BMW blazing past in a trail of gravel dust—which was the same moment she noticed the flame-engulfed house up ahead.

Flooring the gas pedal, she called 911, and against the operator's advice, she ran into the burning farmhouse . . . where she found me slumped over, three steps from the bottom landing.

"I talked to the detective from Willow Branch earlier," I say, inhaling a lungful of salty air as I shove my hands in my pockets. "He said they found part of the knife in the fireplace."

"Well, that's good."

"But," I say with a sigh, "the fire destroyed any DNA evidence there could've been on it . . ."

"Ugh." She lifts a hand to my shoulder, giving it a squeeze. "So frustrating, angel. I know."

I still have moments when I struggle to wrap my head around Merritt's actions. I've always considered myself a decent judge of character—thanks in part to the revolving door of shady people my mother ushered in and out of my younger years. But I thought I had Merritt pinned. I took one look at her and pegged her as a superficial suburban housewife with air for brains and insecurity imbedded into her DNA. And she was generous, kind, and well mannered.

I know now that it was all a facade she hid behind.

A mask of perfection to hide her true ugliness.

From the moment Merritt was apprehended, she's stuck to her story without waver: some made-up tale about me being a jealous, jaded, psychotic first wife who tried to kill her and the kids before taking Luca's life and attempting to go down in flames to skirt any consequences.

I have to admit it's a clever tale, convincing under the right circumstances.

But she made one mistake.

She was wearing my "protection" necklace on her wrist when they took her in . . . and that was the *one* thing she wasn't prepared to explain. It blew a gaping hole in her story. Police had a difficult time believing some distraught postpartum mother could load up her children, fight off a would-be murderer, and somehow manage to steal her attacker's necklace—and then have the audacity to wear it.

Merritt couldn't explain that one away.

But lord knows she tried.

"They have her in custody still," I say. "The judge set bail—the detective thinks he has a soft spot for her since she was a new mother or whatever. But no one's bailed her out yet."

Delphine sniffs. "Good."

From what I heard, no one's claimed Luca's body. Merritt can't do it from behind bars (not that she'd want to at this point), and no other family has stepped forward. I think of him sometimes when I'm lying in bed—his body stiff, lifeless, frozen in some city morgue. Alone. Unwanted. A literal waste of space.

The days of looking over my shoulder are over.

Everything I've ever wanted is finally within arm's reach.

I don't know where their kids are or who's taking care of them. I can only hope they're in capable hands. But what I know for sure is . . . maybe I didn't directly save their lives, but I saved them from a lifetime of being raised by sociopaths.

And that's kind of the same thing.

ACKNOWLEDGMENTS

Every story I've ever written has begun with a seedling of an idea. An intriguing what-if statement. A flash of a scene in my mind's eye. An unanswered question. A mood. A fictional character who demands my attention . . .

And while I may be the one who plants the seeds, an entire team of passionate individuals works tirelessly to cultivate, prune, nourish, sow, and ultimately distribute the fruits of those seeds. It's a fascinating and labor-intensive process each step of the way—but always rewarding.

I'm beyond grateful for my team at Thomas and Mercer, who have once again outdone themselves. To my editors Jessica Tribble Wells and Charlotte Herscher: thank you for your brilliant brainstorming sessions and for pushing me to take this story to the next level. To both Sarahs, Kellie, Lauren, Gracie, and the rest of the T&M team: thank you for all the behind-the-scenes efforts that go into polishing my stories and getting them into the hands of readers all over the world. I am humbled, privileged, and thankful to work with you all.

To my agent, Jill Marsal: thank you for guiding my career in this direction and for your never-ending encouragement.

To Max and Katrina, the keepers of my sanity.

To Neda, PR wizard extraordinaire.

To Shasti, for the gorgeous cover.

To my readers, bloggers, and bookstagrammers who tirelessly promote my books and send me the sweetest emails: thank you so much. Your kind words always brighten my day, and I keep every message.

To my husband, Miss Poots, Marty Graino, and Cozy Cuddles, who settle for scraps of me during crunch time . . . all the love and all the gratitude and all the Disney trips.

Last but not least, special shout-out to Murphy and Milo, whose pug snores served as the writing soundtrack to this book.

ABOUT THE AUTHOR

Photo © 2017 Jill Austin Photography

Minka Kent is the *Washington Post* and *Wall Street Journal* bestselling author of *The Watcher Girl*, *When I Was You*, *The Stillwater Girls*, *The Thinnest Air*, *The Perfect Roommate*, and *The Memory Watcher*. She is a graduate of Iowa State University and resides in Iowa with her husband and three children. For more information, visit www.minkakent.com.